CURSE TWO BIRDS WITH ONE SPELL

A WILDWOOD WITCH MYSTERY: BOOK 8

ELLE ADAMS

On the day of my trial, I wore my lucky Pikachu socks.

Yes, I was aware that they weren't exactly suitable attire for a Head Witch, but I hadn't had a lot of time to do laundry lately, and frankly, I needed all the luck I could get. Mum might have given me a lecture if she'd known, but Mum wasn't there. That was kind of the problem.

Admittedly, with my mother in a coma and my aunt trying to pressure the local witch council into taking away my Head Witch status, a pair of lucky Pikachu socks didn't feel like enough.

Neither did the sceptre. I held the long, pointed instrument in both hands as I walked through the open door to the witches' headquarters, but the all-powerful symbol of the Head Witch's status had as much meaning in my hands as a sword made of rubber. Nothing would convince the people waiting inside the council room a short distance away that I was competent enough to be in charge. Most of them were three times my age and had been sitting on the council since before I was born, and the sole exceptions were the pair of smirking blond witches responsible for challenging me in the first place.

Not good odds.

As I stared into the void—or rather, the council room—Tansy, my red squirrel familiar, curled her fluffy tail around my neck to comfort me. "Come on. Chloe'll help you."

I swivelled to the left, where my assistant, Chloe Watts, beckoned me into my office.

Technically, it wasn't my office any longer, but so far, nobody else had staked their claim, and the steely glint in Chloe's eyes suggested she'd challenge anyone who tried.

"I have a plan," she said.

"I hope it's a good one."

With Chloe, that was a given, but I'd racked my brain all night and eventually concluded that there was about as much chance of me escaping with my job as there was of me developing a sudden proclivity for ballroom dancing.

She nodded. "Yes. I can't postpone the trial, but I can at least slow down the outcome."

"That implies there'll definitely *be* a trial." Even Chloe couldn't work miracles. The trial was mere minutes away, and short of the town being invaded by demons, nothing would stop my aunt's quest to strip me of the sceptre and claim it for herself.

Sweat dampened my palms as I laid the powerful magical instrument that had gained me my title and sealed my fate all in the same instant on my desk. I'd take it with me to the trial, of course, but I was a little worried that my overflowing emotions would cause it to start firing off sparks and set the place ablaze. *I guess that would postpone the trial too.*

Chloe ran her teeth over her lower lip. "The trial itself is just a formality."

"Yeah, a formal challenge to my competence as Head Witch. No big deal." There wasn't a thing I could do to dispute the charges. Saving everyone from a demon didn't count as worthy enough to make an exception.

Chloe lowered her gaze. "There have been other incidents when someone has unsuccessfully challenged the Head Witch. A *lot,* in fact. Jealousy from family members is surprisingly common."

"Is it usually backed up by someone with the entire council on their side?"

Yes, Chloe was far more adept than I was at navigating the world of coven politics, but the council thought I was the worst Head Witch to ever exist, and my only supporter now lay unconscious indefinitely.

Her sister had been waiting for the excuse to wield my many failures against me—including such heinous errors as not being able to remember the names and achievements of every Head Witch to ever exist or answering every letter that crossed my desk the same day—but I'd given her the perfect opportunity when I'd gone to rescue my mother from a rogue Reaper without informing the council, which was supposedly an unforgivable crime. As a result, the council intended to take away the sole weapon that might save us all from a demonic infestation.

That they'd waited until my mother had been put in a coma as a result of being trapped in the afterworld just added insult to injury.

"Stop moping." Grandma's ghostly figure appeared, arms crossed, above her desk. "Throwing a tantrum won't get you anywhere."

"Can't you talk to your youngest daughter?" It was a long shot, I freely admitted, but Aunt Shannon sure as hell wouldn't listen to anyone else.

Grandma gave a hoot of laughter that startled Carmilla, her cat, into waking from her nap on Chloe's desk. "As if she'd listen."

You could have at least tried. The most Grandma had done was refuse to let my aunt or anyone else claim the office while I was under investigation, which I might have taken as proof of her support if I didn't suspect it was more likely that she didn't want anyone moving her belongings around. She didn't even like *me* being in there, but I'd been sure part of her must be angry with my aunt for stealing Mum's position while she was unconscious.

"Then what do you suggest I do?" I enquired.

"Go in there and try not to mess up too badly."

"Thanks." As usual, she was a pinnacle of support and encouragement. Not that I'd expected otherwise.

"I'm sorry," said Chloe when Grandma vanished as swiftly as she'd arrived. "Part of the problem is that we *do* need an interim coven leader while your mother is absent, and nobody else volunteered."

"And they all voted for the person who stole from the coven's finances?" How Aunt Shannon had managed to put together a committee of other council members to declare *me* incompetent as a leader when she'd gone as far as to peddle illegal potions online for cash a few months ago stank like foul play.

Tansy sat upright on my shoulder. "She's blackmailing them, I'm sure."

"Not implausible." How to prove it, though? I had five minutes—no, two—to think of a way out, and my mind was as blank as the paperwork I'd neglected over the past few days while we'd been dealing with the current crisis.

"I'll look into it," Chloe said. "You'd better go. You don't want to be late."

I might have argued that I had a minute, but my time-keeping skills weren't the greatest on a good day, let alone in the middle of a crisis. Frankly, I wasn't sure what I'd even done the previous evening. I might have done more to prepare, but I'd been in too much shock. The whiplash of Mum's injury followed by my aunt's challenge had left me as discombobulated as a squirrel on a raft in the middle of the ocean. Not that Tansy would have appreciated that analogy.

I picked up the sceptre, its heavy weight settling in my hands. *Don't screw this up, Robin.* My ability to control my temper was erratic at the best of times, and my magic reacted to my mood, which was a double recipe for catastrophe when so much depended on my keeping my head in this meeting. No pressure.

My familiar stayed with me until we reached the council room doorway, then she hopped off my shoulder.

"Give them hell, Robin," she said.

I managed a nod before I stepped over the threshold alone. No squirrels inside the council meeting room. I'd broken *that* rule before, but there was no sense in giving my aunt more ammunition to level at me. I surreptitiously glanced down to check that my Pikachu socks weren't showing under my long black cloak and then approached the table.

Aunt Shannon already sat in the seat that was supposed to belong to my mother—another blatant insult—with her daughter Vanessa at her side. My cousin was Aunt Shannon's clone, down to the smirk on her face. I sometimes wondered if she'd ever had a single independent thought in all her life.

Of the other council members, I didn't know any of them particularly well. Wisteria Atkins was the eldest and was morbidly terrified of ghosts, demons, Reapers, and everything associated with them. I could see how Aunt Shannon might have scared her into joining forces, but the others I wasn't so sure about. Belinda Jewell was an elderly witch who wore the same pink headband to every meeting and who generally spent all her time knitting instead of paying attention. To my surprise, though, she was the only person who smiled at me when I took my seat.

The other two—Janine Crow and Laurel Waters—didn't meet my eyes, but they'd noticeably moved their chairs closer to Aunt Shannon's end of the table.

Chloe sat next to me, her notebook and pen at the ready. She might have been my assistant, but her primary role was to take notes and document the meeting. It was nice to imagine that she and Mum had concocted a scheme to challenge Aunt Shannon before the Reaper's betrayal, but I couldn't count on a last-minute rescue.

I had to do this myself.

"Welcome, everyone." I assumed I was meant to start the meeting with the usual meaningless pleasantries, but my aunt cut me off right away.

"As interim coven leader, it's my job to start this meeting," she said. "With the Head Witch under investigation, she forfeits her authority."

I wish you'd forfeit your tongue. My fingers itched to point the sceptre at her, but I laid it down beside the table and sent a silent plea to my magic to stay under control no matter how much my aunt poked at my temper. Showering sparks all over the room would not help my case in the least.

"Then by all means, go ahead," I said. "Say your piece."

"We're here to witness the trial of the current Head Witch," Aunt Shannon began. "As presented by the interim coven leader."

Belinda cleared her throat. "Ah… when were you voted in as interim coven leader? I must have missed it."

I stared at her in disbelief. So did Aunt Shannon. Belinda hadn't put down her knitting, but her words were clear enough.

My aunt made a swift recovery. "To become interim leader requires the support of more than half of the members of the council. Incidentally, that same number of supporters is required to present a challenge to the Head Witch."

Belinda blinked. "Now? With the coven leader in a coma and a demon on the loose?"

I gave her a brief look of gratitude, though I didn't dare say anything aloud in case my aunt took advantage. Belinda was right, though, and it was screamingly obvious that Aunt Shannon hadn't wanted to delay the trial in case my mother woke up first and took back her position. Oh, she didn't *say* that directly, but we all knew it was true.

Nobody else jumped to my defence aside from Belinda, but a tendril of hope unfurled in my chest all the same.

"Yes, now," said Aunt Shannon, though her smile was less wide. "We have everything we need. To start off with, I will offer the reasons for the challenge to the Head Witch's authority, aided by any questions that might be offered by my supporters. Then, the Head Witch will make her own defence, and her allies will add in their own input... if she has any allies present, of course."

My hands clenched under the table. She had me backed into a corner, and she knew it.

"Afterward," she continued, "we will discuss the matter amongst ourselves without the Head Witch being present. Then the verdict will be delivered."

This isn't right. Yes, everything she was doing was perfectly legal, drawing on existing rules straight from the coven handbook, but that didn't make it *right.*

I plastered on a smile. "Fine. Begin."

"So... the challenge," said Aunt Shannon, her smirk back in place. "The primary challenge is that the Head Witch acted inappropriately to her station by failing to inform the rest of the council that a dangerous demon was on the loose in Wildwood Heath. She then made an alliance with a Reaper who turned out to be a criminal and allowed the coven leader to be taken captive then attempted to stage a rescue mission alone. Again, without informing the council."

That's hardly fair. I might have pointed out that Mum had called the Reaper in the first place, that neither of us had known Linnea would turn out to be a traitor—but Mum was in a coma and unable to defend herself *or* me.

As for Aunt Shannon, it couldn't have been more obvious that she was having the time of her life listing all my inadequacies for the world to hear. I wanted to punch her in the nose. Unfortunately, that would have fallen into the category of an inappropriate response in a coven meeting. Instead, I clenched my fists and occupied myself with the mental image of a bucket of animal dung upending itself on her head.

It didn't quite work. Anger buzzed in my veins, and the loud birdsong outside the window indicated the local wildlife had picked up on the magic fizzing from my skin, but I managed to hold back an outburst by sheer force of will. Mercifully, the sceptre gave no response to my emotions. Maybe it'd picked up on my silent pleas after all.

When I was allowed to speak, I rose upright. I hadn't practised giving a statement, but it wasn't hard to remember the events I had to recount. Every minute was seared into my brain. The false Reaper's betrayal. The demon's attack. Mum's disappearance. And, yes, the part when I'd decided not to tell the council before I went after her. If I had, Mum might not have survived.

"I'm sure that if any of your family members had been taken hostage, you'd have reacted the same," I said to finish my account. "As it is, I was able to save her before she lost her life. The demon responsible for the attack…"

"…is gone, I believe," Aunt Shannon said, her tone so cheerful she practically sang the words. "If you've finished with your account, it's time for me and my supporters to ask any outstanding questions."

"Of course." I gave a strained smile. "Go ahead."

"It never occurred to you to ask for backup?" she began. "Rather than pursuing the false Reaper alone? Surely, that would have given your mother a better chance of survival."

"I had my brother. He's the head of the police and has dealt with demons before." Kind of. In truth, nobody had been prepared for a *Reaper* to turn against us, and I doubted any of the people in this room would have fared any better than I had.

"The Head Witch must always ask the coven for support before the police," said Wisteria in her hoarse voice.

Would you have offered any support? Wisteria was terrified of ghosts. I bit back my urge to point out the obvious, but surely, everyone in the room knew she wouldn't have gone into the afterworld to help get my mother out. Neither would anyone else in this room, come to that.

Aunt Shannon tutted. "Sad to say, it's a noticeable pattern. Since the new Head Witch was appointed, we've seen a definite decline in standards and procedures."

If I'd been a squirrel, my tail would have been standing on end in indignation. *Standards and procedures?* I thought most of those standards were nonsensical bureaucracy designed to stop anything actually getting done, and they were about as effective in a crisis as a small bucket on a sinking ship. Would she rather the whole town had been taken over by demons?

"I thought the challenge to my leadership was about my actions on that specific day," I said pointedly. "There were extenuating circumstances. A demon possessed several citizens of Wildwood Heath, and a rogue Reaper attacked the town. Some might say this is a time when our coven needs to work closely together, not split into factions."

"This is a time for strong leadership," Aunt Shannon corrected. "Not lies and excuses."

And you've never lied for your own benefit? With every word she said, my temper rose higher. This was a waste of time on all levels, but the real kick in the face was that she'd done far worse than I had, and everyone had seemingly forgotten. Mum… God, I wished she was here. She might have made a habit of nitpicking at my inadequacies, but she at least didn't have a convenient case of amnesia when it came to her younger sister. *I* knew I was far from beyond reproach, but this was ridiculous.

Really, it came down to one immutable fact. In the end, I was never going to be good enough for these people. Never.

"Now for the verdict," she concluded. "As stated, we'll discuss the subject amongst ourselves as a council, and we'll deliver our decision in an hour. How does that sound?"

I bit back my instinctive *Screw you.* "Perfectly acceptable."

No miracles presented themselves. Chloe rose to her feet and followed me out of the room with her head bowed.

"I thought," I said out of the corner of my mouth, "you had a plan."

"I do."

"Does it involve them taking the sceptre away?" I hissed. "And letting her take Mum's title?"

The latter, she couldn't have stopped, and Mum had shown no signs of waking up so far. Being trapped in the afterworld wasn't the kind of affliction you could cure with regular magic. I'd even asked Maura—the sole Reaper I'd met who *hadn't* turned out to be a massive traitor—but she'd shaken her head and told me that there was nothing she could do either.

Linnea herself was in jail, or so I thought. She'd been arrested by the Wardens, but they might have handed her over to the Reaper Council. I didn't know. Thanks to my aunt's scheming, I'd been unable to check to make sure she'd been put somewhere she couldn't harm anyone else.

"They won't," Chloe said. "They might be able to remove

your Head Witch title, but if the sceptre chooses you again, they won't be able to do anything to challenge the decision."

"*That's* your plan?" My tone was sharper than I'd intended, but I'd assumed her plan involved my aunt not having a chance to even *try* to claim the sceptre.

Chloe flinched. "The sceptre chose you. There's no reason it wouldn't do so again."

"There are plenty of reasons." Sceptres could change their minds—metaphorically speaking—and while my aunt was at the bottom of my list of options, it wouldn't have surprised me if she found a way to exclude all other possible candidates.

Mostly, I felt a fool for forgetting that the sceptre had been her target from the start. At first, she'd seemingly accepted her defeat, but that she'd been preparing a coup all along shouldn't have been a surprise.

Upon entering my office, Chloe turned to me. "Robin, your aunt knows the sceptre will choose you again if she gives it the option. She won't be able to take it away permanently. That's our loophole."

"That's not a loophole." Hardly. The sceptre had nobody else to choose, which was why it'd picked the family screw-up above all other options. Who was to say it wouldn't pick my aunt if she locked me out of the room? "What if she has me arrested or just locked in another room when the sceptre picks its next wielder? Can you guarantee it won't go with the only available choice?"

Her mouth parted. "I…"

She doesn't know. The tendril of hope in my chest withered and died. "You know what happens if she wins."

We'd all die. I wasn't even exaggerating. Two demons wanted me dead, one of which had fled town while possessing Leona, former assistant to the Henbane Coven's leader. My aunt's coup would paint a neon target on the town, which she must surely know, but her own ambitions won out over common sense.

Chloe turned her attention to the desk, upon which a neat stack of books sat. "I'm certain the sceptre *will* pick you, but I can take another look at the rule book and check for any more loopholes to delay your aunt's takeover attempt."

I managed a grateful smile. "Thanks."

Would I be able to rely on mere bureaucracy to drag out the matter and buy some time? Perhaps, but that time might not be long enough no matter what. I wasn't in any way ready to face the demons, but my aunt had added a new layer of urgency to the quest the sceptre had given me. There was no hunting demons while I was trapped here, playing my aunt's silly games.

I have to get her off my back. Somehow.

2

I couldn't stay in the office a moment longer. I needed some air. Hoping that Aunt Shannon and the council were too busy dissecting my inadequacies to notice, I left the room and made for the front door.

Tansy met me outside. "How was it?"

"How do you think?" I lowered my head. "Aunt Shannon has the entire council in her pocket. Except possibly Belinda, but she's being shouted down by the others."

"Carmilla said they can't take the sceptre right away," Tansy said. "I asked."

I didn't look behind me to see if Grandma's cat was paying attention. "I know. Chloe said the sceptre will pick me if it comes down to it. But what if Aunt Shannon solves the problem by locking me out of the room or something? There's no way she didn't consider that angle."

Tansy jumped onto my shoulder. "It's not like you to give up that easily."

"I haven't. I just can't think clearly in here." Being a downer wasn't my style. To survive the constant setbacks that I'd experienced in my lifetime as the family screw-up, I'd had to develop some airtight coping mechanisms, but the gradual wearing down of my sense of stability over the past week, coupled with my mother's coma, had knocked me sideways. And while I knew my aunt's challenge to my leadership was nothing but a cover for her own ambitions, it drove home the point that some of the council would rather see the entire coven go up in flames than see me in charge. I mean, how could that not be a massive blow to even the most inflated of egos?

"Then talk to Rowan." Tansy flicked my ear with her tail. "She'll give you a pep talk, and Chloe will come up with a winning strategy while we're gone."

"I hope you're right." Spying Chloe herself behind me, I swivelled around. "I'll be back before the verdict. Don't worry."

"All right, but please… set an alarm." She knew my ineptitude at timekeeping better than most people, so I did as she asked before I left the building with my familiar.

I'd promised to give Rowan an update when the trial was over, and she wouldn't be expecting me to show up yet, but staying in the office to await the verdict with Grandma's ghost and her equally cantankerous cat did not appeal in the least. Besides, getting some fresh air might blow the cobwebs out of my brain and replace them with some inspiration.

On a clear day like this, with sunlight beaming down between leafy branches and onto the roofs of the picturesque streets, the reminder was stark that I'd always loved Wildwood Heath itself. If not for my expected role in the coven, which had rubbed against me like too-small shoes, I might have stayed. Those expectations had multiplied by a thousandfold since I'd been chosen as Head Witch, and if I'd been in this position a few years ago, I might have made a different choice.

Now, there was only one option. I'd fight to stay in Wildwood Heath with everything I had inside me.

Tansy made a rude noise when I'd finished recounting my aunt's humiliating trial. "I think it's safe to say your aunt blackmailed the rest of the council into backing her. What does she have on them, I wonder?"

"I don't really care, to be honest." I doubted anyone on the council would admit to being blackmailed or bribed, and Aunt Shannon would be too clever to leave evidence exposed after we'd caught her in the act with those illegal potions. While part of me had considered sending Tansy to snoop around her office and see what she unearthed, my aunt would never make the same mistake twice.

"How many people does she actually need to have on her side to win the trial?" Tansy went on. "There are eight members. Does that mean she needs at least five votes, including herself?"

"Yes, and she has…" I counted them off on my fingers. "Exactly five. Of the other three, one is Mum, and the other is me, and I'm pretty sure we don't count."

"She and Vanessa are two of the five, and they don't count either." Tansy persisted. "What about the other three?"

"Wisteria… all I know about her is that she's terrified of ghosts," I replied. "Maybe Aunt Shannon threatened to set Grandma on her."

Tansy snorted. "Let's see what Rowan says."

We'd reached the main street, which contained most of the local shops, including Were's My Coffee? The café where Rowan worked was quieter at this hour, and when I walked in, I found my younger cousin seated at a table like a regular customer.

Upon seeing me, she bolted upright. "Robin. I expected you later."

I hugged her, grimacing when her tarantula familiar's

hairy leg brushed against my face from up her sleeve. "I'm just here for a bit. The council's having a private discussion on the verdict, so I thought I'd get outside while I could."

"Are you okay?"

I shrugged. What was there to even say?

Rowan waited a heartbeat, realised she wasn't getting a reply, and said, "My mother can't win the trial. She *can't*. Nobody should vote for her. She's the worst possible person for the job. I can't think of anyone I'd less like to be Head Witch at a time of crisis."

"Worse than Leona?" Tansy put in. "Or Tiffany? Remember her?"

"Does Leona even count as a person anymore?" Rowan dropped her voice, though the only other customers sat on the other side of the café and were engrossed in conversation without paying us any attention. "As for Tiffany, my mother should be behind bars alongside her."

"I don't disagree." I pulled up a chair at her table. "She's got the council under her thumb. Except Belinda, Mum, and me, but I don't need to explain how little use the three of us are."

I summarised the meeting after I ordered a latte to go, needing all the fortitude I could get. Tansy went to chase pigeons near the door while Rowan and I sat and talked.

"There has to be something you can do," Rowan insisted. "You're *Head Witch*."

"Trust me, I'm aware." I lowered my gaze to my coffee cup. "She scoured the rule book thoroughly and came up with every possible way to get rid of me. Chloe thinks I'll be fine because the sceptre will just pick me again, but that's not a guarantee, and I wouldn't be surprised if your mother found a way to exclude me from the ceremony altogether."

Rowan scrunched up her forehead. "She can't *force* the

sceptre to accept her instead of you. If you aren't there, it won't pick anyone."

"If anyone's persistent enough to try, it's her." I sipped my drink. "Tansy thinks I'm being a downer, and so does Grandma, but if even Chloe can't figure out how to best her, what are my odds?"

"Better than you think," she said. "The sceptre will pick you again. My mother got possessed by the demon. You didn't. Objectively, you're the better choice."

"The rest of the council doesn't see it that way." Maybe Tansy was right, and my aunt had won them over via subterfuge, but how would I prove it and to whom? The council was supposed to be in charge of making those decisions and wasn't accountable to the police, to the other magical authorities, or anyone else. Strangely, nobody else seemed to have a problem with that.

"The council shouldn't have the power to unseat a Head Witch," she said. "Surely, only the other Head Witches can have that authority. Hey, can't you call Jemima?"

"What, and beg her to come to my rescue?" For all I knew, there was a rule forbidding that, and besides, begging another Head Witch for help would hardly help the lacking impression of my own competence.

"The other Head Witches outrank my mother," she said. "At least consider asking her. Jemima's friends with your mum, isn't she?"

"Mum wouldn't want me to tell anyone." I sipped more coffee, though the caffeine didn't bring the level of clarity I'd hoped. "Not doing things by the book is why I'm being challenged in the first place."

"It's also why you've lived longer than some Head Witches, I bet." She remained unconvinced. "Seriously. You're the one who taught me not to give up my principles even when others tried their best to convince me otherwise.

I'll never regret leaving my mother's house, no matter how much it cost me."

"I know." I crumpled the empty coffee cup in my hand. "It's not me who'll pay the price if I lose my title, though. The demons want revenge on the whole family, and I'll have a hell of a lot more difficulty stopping Leona without the sceptre."

She drummed her fingers on the table. "What about the Wardens? I saw your brother talking to the ones who came to arrest Linnea."

"The Wardens?" I thought back to our brief encounter at the police station. "I guess they have some expertise at fighting magical monsters, but the Reapers were supposed to be able to help, too, and look how that turned out."

"Yeah." She chewed on her lower lip. "I don't have any other ideas as to how to handle the demons, but I *do* have a possible way to stop my mother. It's risky, though."

"Risky in what way?"

"Call your favourite reporters," she said. "Ask them to pry into my mother's history and unearth a story that will make her quest to become Head Witch impossible."

My mouth fell open. "No way."

"I didn't think you'd like that idea."

"They aren't even working for the *Blue Moon* anymore," I pointed out. "They went into sports journalism."

"I bet they'd jump at the chance to help the Head Witch," she pressed. "They already *have* all the gossip on our family from the stories printed over the years."

"Most of which were abject nonsense."

"Not all of them." Her eyes gleamed. "There's some real dirt to be unearthed there, I bet."

"It'll also throw the rest of us under the bus as well." I'd made it clear to a certain pair of overly inquisitive reporters that I wouldn't talk to them any further after our last interview, and letting them back into my life would bring more problems than it solved, especially if they found out my mother was in a coma and my leadership was being challenged. "It's far more likely to backfire on me. They'll want to know all about the trial as soon as they find out."

"Not if we keep that part a secret."

"We can't, not from them."

"You'd be surprised."

I shook my head. "No. We'll think of something else." What, I had no idea.

My phone alarm went off, telling me my time was up, so I dragged myself to my feet.

"It's already time?" Concern flickered in Rowan's eyes.

"Yeah, I set an alarm to make sure I'm not late back to the office. Can't miss out on the trial of a lifetime." Despite my flippant tone, my anxiety spiked. Was this the last time I'd drop by the café as a Head Witch? How long before everyone in the village knew I'd been dismissed in disgrace? Aunt Shannon had kept the knowledge confined to the coven so far, but that would change soon enough. And when word spread, the press would inevitably find out too.

Maybe Rowan was right and I should preemptively get in touch to win them to my side before my aunt took away that option, but they moved fast enough that the news would be all over the tabloids by tomorrow morning. I had no doubt of that.

Without any other options, Tansy and I left the café and returned to the coven headquarters. When the grand house came into view, I approached with the trepidation of someone climbing the gallows and nearly walked straight into Chloe in the doorway.

"Robin." She beckoned me into the office. "I was going to come looking for you. I figured it out."

"What?" My heart jumped. "You worked out how to stop her?"

"Not quite." She darted through the office door and smiled at me. "But I did figure out how to stall for time."

"How much time?"

Tansy scampered over and jumped onto the desk as I closed the door behind me.

"The coven leader being incapacitated allows for special circumstances," she said. "I forgot to check the fine print. When a coven leader is taken out of action, there *does* need to be a vote on an interim coven leader, but that leader also isn't allowed to make any decisions that will significantly affect the coven during the first month of her leadership."

My mouth dropped open. "The first month? Are you sure?"

She nodded eagerly. "Yes. It's pretty clear. I'm guessing your aunt didn't look that up. She assumed she'd be allowed to act as a full coven leader from the get-go."

"You're a genius." I allowed myself a smile, but I refrained from any more inappropriate behaviour like dancing around the office. We hadn't won yet, and my aunt was still inside the meeting room, waiting for me to screw up.

A flush spread across Chloe's cheekbones. "I just thought… well, if we can delay the decision for a month and your mother wakes up, we won't need to worry about your aunt trying again."

"There's no guarantee." Some of my euphoria faded. "We can't count on her waking up in time to fix this."

I also hated that I had to think of her fate in those terms, as if her intervening to save my neck was more important than her actual recovery from the rogue Reaper's attack. Thanks to Aunt Shannon, I hadn't even been able to help take care of her. You'd have thought *one* other person on the council would have some concern for their coven leader's recovery.

"You truly have a knack for bringing the mood down." Grandma came drifting out from behind a filing cabinet. "Isn't it enough that you get a chance to try again?"

"Try and do what, hunt the demons?" *Your* demons, I should have said. She was the one whose untimely murder had saddled me with all her responsibilities and little of the support. The council would never have questioned *her* competence.

"To win the council back to your side, of course," she said. "Frankly, I think you ought to be looking into why that Janine Crow threw her support in with my younger daughter. She doesn't even *like* Shannon."

"Really?" I frowned. "Well, she evidently likes her more than she likes me. Or thinks she'll do a better job. One or the other."

"Or she was blackmailed," Tansy added. "Why not ask her directly? She won't be expecting that."

"You can't just *ask* someone if they were blackmailed and expect them to admit to it."

"There's nothing wrong with employing a little blackmail of your own," Grandma put in.

"*Grandma.*" I *hoped* she wasn't being serious. "Chloe, please tell me you don't agree with her."

"We never discussed blackmail," she objected. "That said, it might be worth talking to Janine and asking why she decided to support your aunt's bid for power. You'll have time to do that once the trial is delayed."

Yes, and what of the demons? Two months remained before Samhain, the night on which the sceptre was traditionally supposed to choose a new wielder, and I'd been counting on that ceremony to set me free from the obligation of being Head Witch. In part, I'd only endured my new status for this long because I knew I'd be allowed to quit when the sceptre chose someone else—or when I banished Grandma's demons. Whatever came first. Yet with my aunt's coup came renewed certainty that the former wasn't an option yet.

The demons had to be banished, and for whatever reason, the sceptre had chosen me as its wielder to defend the coven. Whatever other rules I'd broken, I'd never turn my back on that mission.

"She's right," Chloe said anxiously. "Your mother would be more than happy to take over from you when the time comes, but whatever that Reaper did to her…"

"I know." My heart twisted into knots. What if she never woke up? If I had to remain at her comatose side while my aunt rampaged over her legacy for months or years … no, I wouldn't allow it. While I didn't know who would wield the sceptre after me if Mum wasn't an option, that question was firmly in the "later" category. Stopping my aunt came first.

"Look on the bright side," Carmilla said without opening her eyes. "If the demons kill you, you won't have to worry about any of this."

"Really helpful." I gave Grandma's half-bald cat a disgruntled look. "The Reapers were supposed to help me deal with the demons and not turn against me. Have either of you remembered what you did that upset Linnea so much?"

Chloe sucked in a breath, but Grandma pretended not to hear.

"Grandma?" I asked. "She claimed that our family killed her mother."

"I certainly did not," Grandma huffed. "How could you accuse me of such a thing?"

"I'm not accusing—" I broke off when she vanished in a gust of air that knocked a stack of papers sideways. "Oh, come on."

"You have to go back to the meeting room." Chloe

hastened to rescue the papers before they scattered on the floor. "It'll be fine. I'll bring the rule book, and I'll be ready to speak."

"Dammit." My nerves spiked, sharp and intense, and I took in several long breaths to steady myself.

Focus, Robin. You've been given a lifeline. Don't screw this up.

Tansy jumped onto the table and flicked her tail. "Go on, Robin. You can knock her off her pedestal."

"I sure hope so."

I left the room with Chloe close behind me. We entered the council meeting room to find little had changed since we'd left. Belinda was still knitting, while Aunt Shannon sat in Mum's seat. Vanessa, Wisteria, and Laurel had all angled their chairs towards hers, but Janine hadn't. Did that mean she wasn't in on the plan? Grandma had said the pair didn't like one another. Maybe I could tug on that thread if I had the chance.

I retook my seat and cleared my throat. "Shall we begin?"

"The verdict is in," Aunt Shannon said. "The council has voted to remove the Head Witch from her position."

I tried to keep my face blank, waiting for Chloe to speak, while my aunt continued. "To start off with, the sceptre will be handed to the interim coven leader and then presented to a new wielder in a ceremony—"

"That isn't possible." Chloe spoke up, her voice soft but clear. "According to magical law, when an interim coven leader is chosen, she is not allowed to make any decisions of this magnitude for the first month of her leadership or until a permanent replacement is found."

My aunt blinked, her mouth falling open. "I beg your pardon?"

"It's in the rule book." Chloe held it up. "Interim coven leaders have some level of authority, but no permanent decisions are allowed to be made, and I would assume that removing a Head Witch's title would qualify under that rule."

"It would," added Belinda.

The others gaped at Chloe as though surprised she'd have the nerve. Vanessa looked as though she'd opened a birthday present and found a live rat in place of a gift. Despite my lingering nerves, I suppressed a grin.

Aunt Shannon was a little more composed, with a hint of polite incredulity fixed on her face. "Until a permanent replacement is found, you say?"

"There's a procedure for that too," said Chloe. "Like I said, it's in the rule book, but it's not possible for you to take the sceptre from Robin today."

A disbelieving silence filled the room. I took that as my cue to speak. "Under those rules, the Head Witch keeps the sceptre, and the final decision is put on hold. If the interim coven leader wants to issue the challenge again in a month's time, she is welcome to."

Aunt Shannon's pale face flushed a little. "Delaying the trial's outcome will achieve nothing."

We both know that's not true. "You're welcome to try again in a month. Is there anything else you wanted to discuss while we're here?"

Nobody answered. The rest of the council members didn't look *happy* about the delay, but they had no audible objections either. Belinda, though too busy knitting to look up at the rest of the table, wore the slightest smile on her face.

"Then the meeting is over," I finished. "You may leave."

We did it. I'd delayed the verdict a whole month. Yes, Mum was still in a coma, and the demons remained at large, but we'd won time to figure out a solution.

And I intended to make every extra minute count.

3

With the meeting over, the rest of the day would have been mine... if not for one slight issue. The sole perk of being under investigation had been that I'd had to put everything else on hold, including the veritable mountain of paperwork that landed on my desk every day. Said paperwork would be waiting for me back in the office, so I resignedly walked there with Chloe.

"What now?" I asked her. "Do I just... go on as if nothing has happened?"

"I think you're entitled to the rest of the day off." Tansy sat on my desk inside the office. "I take it your plan worked?"

"It did." I scanned the office in case Grandma had reappeared, but she remained absent. Probably avoiding any future questions that I might throw at her concerning a certain Reaper. "Chloe, how much paperwork did I miss?"

A slightly embarrassed pause followed. "I... may have already handled it myself."

"Chloe." Honestly. She went way above what the coven paid her, especially as she'd also been trying to figure out how to get me off the hook for this trial. I should have known never to underestimate her. "You know what, we'll *both* take the afternoon off. I think we've earned it."

I needed to give Rowan an update on the trial, along with pretty much everyone else in my life who I hadn't had a proper chance to talk to before my aunt had issued her challenge. Such as Harvey and Dad.

"Go on." Tansy jumped on Chloe's shoulder and gave her a gentle nudge with her paws. "The Head Witch has spoken."

I'm still Head Witch... for now. In truth, my main motivation for taking a half day was out of a desire to *not* be in the same office as my conspicuously absent predecessor. If she refused to answer my questions, I'd return the favour.

"Grandma's memory certainly is selective when she wants it to be," I remarked to Tansy as we left the building. "How can she have forgotten angering a Reaper enough for her to want our entire family dead? What's the goal in keeping me in the dark?"

"She's been unreliable since she became a ghost," Tansy replied. "Forget her. We need to celebrate."

I checked the time. "Harvey won't be out of work until later."

Piper would be around somewhere, but I didn't feel like going home. And Rowan, of course, would be at the café.

"What about your brother?" suggested Tansy. "He'll want to know you escaped your fate."

I pulled a face. "He will, but he'll also rain on my parade by coming up with another stack of reasons why I'm screwed."

"Might he have something to say about your grandmother not answering your questions?" she reminded me. "I bet he will."

That was true. "Okay. Let's see if my brother can jog her memory."

We followed the road to the centre of the town, this time

heading for the police station. The small brick building was one of the handful equipped with modern features like automatic doors, which slid open to let us inside. Julian, the receptionist, half rose from his chair as I walked in. "Ah… it's you, Robin."

"It is." Did he sound surprised? Yes… yes, he did. How much had Ramsey told him? "Here to see my brother."

I walked to Ramsey's office and knocked on the door.

"Robin," Ramsey answered, his blond hair combed flat and his suit as impeccable as ever. "What are you doing here?"

"Visiting my brother to tell him I'm off the hook?" I spied his hedgehog familiar, Prickles, sitting on the desk with his paws folded underneath him. Neither of them showed any visible surprise or relief at my arrival. "Chloe managed to postpone the trial for a month."

"I know. She told me."

"She didn't tell *me* she told you." I could always count on my brother to bring me down from my high. "We have a month—or as long as it takes Mum to wake up from her coma—so I figured I should work on a plan for what to do in the interim. You know, about the demons. The rogue Reaper. All that stuff."

"Really?" He cocked a brow. "I'm surprised you want to take action this soon rather than celebrating your victory."

"Everyone else is at work. As well you know." My good mood had thoroughly deflated. "I hoped you'd be happy for me. Just a little."

The faintest sigh escaped. "I am, Robin, but as you just reminded both of us, I'm supposed to be working."

"All right." I recalled the reason I'd originally come here. "I also thought you should know that Grandma still doesn't remember why Leona hates our family so much. Have you talked to her since Mum… you know."

"No," he said. "I imagine she wanted you to focus on the trial."

"She's still avoiding me," I said. "As for the trial, her only advice was that I should blackmail Aunt Shannon's supporters into switching sides."

My brother's mouth puckered as though he'd accidently sat on Prickles. "You most certainly should not."

"I never said it was a sensible idea." I turned to my familiar, only to find that she'd run outside to chase a pigeon at some point during our conversation. "Tansy thinks Aunt Shannon blackmailed them into taking her side in the first place and that I ought to try to find proof."

"How would you go about that?" His mouth turned down at the corners. "I wouldn't waste your time wondering about how she gathered her supporters."

"And Rowan suggested calling the press and asking them to dig up dirt on Aunt Shannon."

Ramsey's face went as red as the police station's brick walls. "What?"

"I knew you wouldn't like that," I said. "I didn't say I agreed with her either. I just thought I'd pass on an idea you might like more than blackmail."

"That *is* blackmail."

"What, of Aunt Shannon?" I tilted my head. "Hasn't she tried to do the same thing to the rest of us countless times? Besides, Clarice and Speck aren't with the *Blue Moon* any longer. If I called them to ask a favour…"

"Out of the question," he said sharply. "Protecting the coven and the town should be your priority."

"I wasn't *actually* going to call them," I said. "Though if I'm going to protect the town, it'll be a lot easier without most of the council in Aunt Shannon's pocket."

"There's nothing the council can do to help you."

"Did you just say the council was useless?" I mean, he

wasn't wrong, but he'd never been that open in his criticism of them before.

"Of course not," he said, "but they aren't trained to fight demons. Neither are you, for that matter, despite your recent experiences."

"Ouch." I lifted a hand to my chest as though he'd mortally wounded me. "I realise that, but our alternative is waiting for Mum to wake up, and that might take months. Linnea betrayed us, remember? The Reapers aren't an option."

"The Wardens are."

Right. Rowan had brought them up as a suggestion, but I'd forgotten. "Have you heard from them since they arrested Linnea?"

"No, but I can set up a meeting," he said. "I expect they have ways of tracking demons. I'll ask."

That was unexpected. "They can find Leona?"

"Potentially."

"And help us banish the demon?" Would it really be that easy? I doubted it. "They aren't Reapers, though. They don't have any special powers designed to deal with the dead."

"Contacting the Reapers themselves is out of the question, and the Wardens are the next available choice," he said. "As they're the ones who took Linnea into custody, they might be able to verify what led to her going astray too. They aren't under the same secrecy agreements as the Reapers are."

"You know… you bring up a good point." He also spoke as if he'd come up with the idea a while ago, not in the last five minutes. "Do you think they can find out if what Linnea claimed was true? Grandma won't say a word, but I have a hard time believing anyone in our coven murdered her mother. Even accidentally."

His eyes narrowed a little. "I wouldn't advise you to share

that information with them, but they'll likely have any demon-related incidents in the area on record."

"That's something, at least." They'd be able to find our elusive demon, and if they found out the truth about Linnea in the process, so much the better.

"I'll contact them," he said. "Can you refrain from making any calls to the press before then? We need to keep this quiet."

"Of course." I hadn't intended on calling them right away —or at all if an alternative showed up—but it was nice to have a direction to follow.

I dropped in at the café to pass on the good news to Rowan. She was busy with the lunchtime shift, so I grabbed a sandwich and gave her a thumbs-up while I paid. There weren't any tables free, so I left her to wrangle both customers and the new intern she was training, who seemed incapable of holding a coffee cup the right way up.

"I'm surprised they have her training someone else already," I said to Tansy as I walked out of the café, munching on my sandwich. "She's fairly new herself."

"Yes, but didn't one of her former colleagues get arrested?"

"Fair point." I also kept forgetting that while Rowan was comparatively new to her job, she'd got the position shortly after I'd been chosen as Head Witch, and it felt like that particular burden had rested on my head for a decade. "All right, let's see if Piper's around."

The answer was no; as it turned out, Mum's familiar had chased her out of the garden to stop her from touching the rose beds while his witch was in a coma. That seemed harsh, but Horace had been in a tetchy mood since Mum had been confined to her room, and he had taken to prowling the landing outside her bedroom door and stonily watching anyone else who went in. I lasted all of five minutes in the house before I took off to visit Dad instead. That always cheered me up.

Dad's cottage, which he shared with his new wife, Jessica, and her two kids from her previous marriage, sat just inside the Wildwood in a clearing framed by leafy trees. Shifters preferred territory close to the woods, where they could shift and run to their hearts' content. I could see the two kids running around the garden covered in mud, and when Tansy climbed the fence, they pursued her with cries of delight.

While they chased her around, I went into the house and filled Dad in on the events of the trial. Not everything, but enough that he knew I wasn't in imminent danger of being replaced. Dad's obvious relief at my newfound freedom was a welcome change from my brother's reaction, that was for sure.

"I'm glad." Dad smiled at me. "It's incredibly unjust, what your aunt was trying to do. She's obnoxious."

"She is," I agreed. "Chloe has managed to postpone Aunt Shannon's ambitions for the time being, but my instinct tells me she'll try something else at the first opportunity. I need to be ready."

"Sounds like Chloe is more than on top of things."

"I'm glad one of us is," I said. "Grandma suggested black-mail, and…"

As for Rowan? Her idea of calling the reporters had nestled in the back of my mind, and I found myself compelled to ask Dad for his input.

"Blackmail?" he echoed. "What, of your aunt?"

"Yes, and Rowan suggested calling the press and asking if they had any sordid stories on her that would send her supporters fleeing."

"That'd be risky," he said. "You also worked really hard to get rid of those reporters, didn't you?"

I should have expected that response, as Dad above all

had suffered the brunt of media speculation during his marriage to and eventual divorce from Mum. The press had gleefully dissected everything about his life and held it up to scrutiny, and if anyone would be able to offer me an honest opinion on whether it was worth poking that manticore, it was him.

At the same time, Aunt Shannon had a plethora of skeletons lurking inside her closet. Who deserved to have her secrets exposed more than she did?

"Yeah, I know." I grimaced. "Ramsey said no way, but right now, it's a technicality that's saving me from losing my position, nothing more. My aunt will persist until Mum wakes up—or until someone takes action that makes it impossible for her to stay as interim coven leader."

"Does your brother have an opinion?"

"He's setting up a meeting with the Wardens." I didn't mention the demons. Dad had had a close call at their hands already, and nobody needed the reminder.

His expression clouded all the same. "I assume he knows what he's doing, but... please be careful, Robin. What happened to your mother might easily have happened to you instead."

"I know." To say Dad and Mum had a complicated relationship was an understatement. Their divorce had been amicable on his end, but Mum had had to make the whole thing overly complicated by bringing the coven's reputation into it and had also practically refused to let Ramsey and me see Dad at all during the proceedings. As a result, Dad and Ramsey had only just recently begun to repair their relationship.

The press certainly hadn't helped matters, but what other way was there to unseat Aunt Shannon than by wielding her own reputation against her? As to whether that would make me just as bad as she was... I couldn't answer that question. It seemed impossible not to get my hands dirty if I wanted to prevent the sceptre from falling into her grasp.

"It's up to you, of course." Dad gave me a hug. "I'm on your side. Never doubt that."

I gave him a smile. "I know that too."

Dad was always a hundred percent on my side, and I always walked away from the cottage in a better mood. Today, I stayed until the sun began to sink in the sky and I had no choice but to drag myself back home.

When I did get back to the house, Ramsey hadn't shown up yet either. Burying himself in work to avoid facing Mum, at a guess. Not that I blamed him. At least I had a date with Harvey that night to distract myself. I'd already sent him a quick text telling him I was off the hook for the trial for the time being, but he'd been teaching at the local academy all afternoon and hadn't been able to come and see me.

I changed out of my muddy clothes into a nice skirt and top and walked to the Fox's Den, the local pub and our favourite dating spot. My heart lifted when I set eyes on Harvey. His broad arms offered a comforting hug, and I gladly leaned into his embrace until Tansy interrupted by jumping on my head.

"Sorry." I shooed her off and entered the pub alongside Harvey. "I think she's a bit on edge still."

He peered at my face as we sat down at our usual table. "You're okay, though?"

I nodded. "Yeah. The short version of the story is I'm off the hook for a month thanks to a loophole Chloe found in the rule book. Other than that, please don't ask me to relive the whole experience. I've already done it four times."

"I won't," he said easily. "I'm sorry, though. Your aunt shouldn't have put you through that with all the crap you already have going on."

"So am I." I heaved a sigh. "I don't want to think this was

avoidable, that I could have stopped her, but I do wonder if I might have paid more attention to her scheming."

"You couldn't have known," he insisted. "You had your priorities in the right place. It's not your fault she took advantage. I'm glad your assistant was able to come through for you."

I smiled. "Yeah, Chloe's amazing. I'll have to talk to Mum about giving her a pay raise when she wakes up."

When. I had to use that word, not *if.* She *would* wake up.

"That's got to be a weight off your mind," he said. "I know the trial's not delayed indefinitely, but your aunt shouldn't be allowed to take away the sceptre without being challenged."

"No." I tapped on the menu to order a drink. "Chloe's other plan was to let my aunt go ahead and redo the ceremony, under the assumption that the sceptre would choose me again. I'm not sure I want to stake the entire future of the coven on those odds."

"The sceptre picked you for a reason, and that hasn't changed, has it?"

"Theoretically, no." I lowered my gaze, pretending to be immersed in the menu and wishing I hadn't alluded to the disembodied elephant in the room. Demons were kind of a mood killer. "And my aunt's already proven she can't handle it when she got possessed."

"Exactly." He reached for my hand and took it. "I have faith in you."

"Wish you were on the council," I quipped. "Actually, I don't. It'd suck all the joy out of your life."

He flashed me a grin. "I thought team meetings discussing finances were bad enough. I had one of those after work. That's why I couldn't come and meet you sooner."

"Fun." I selected my favourite pasta dish from the menu. "I can't believe I'm celebrating having another month of this."

"A month," he repeated. "When would the sceptre usually pick a new owner? Samhain, right?"

"Yes." My mood yo-yoed back down again. "If the demon isn't gone by then, I'm stuck with the sceptre for another year."

Especially if Mum didn't wake up, but I didn't voice that part aloud.

He ordered his own meal. "I know that's not what you wanted, but… maybe it's not a bad thing to have a bit more time to prepare."

He had a point, but my whole body rebelled against the notion of being trapped in the role for another twelve months, even if it was preferable to my aunt getting the job. "It'd help if Mum woke up."

He squeezed my hand again. "I'm sure she'll be fine. How's your brother doing, anyway?"

"Throwing himself into work, same as usual," I said. "Oh, and he thinks the Wardens might be able to help, since the Reapers turned out to be a bust. He said he'd set up a meeting with them."

"Oh, good," he said. "Didn't they arrest that Reaper? Was that them?"

"Yeah." I fidgeted, not wanting to get onto *that* subject either. Then again, maybe he could offer some advice where my brother had been unwilling. "She made some bizarre accusations against my coven, and my grandmother seems to have inconveniently forgotten ever having met her. I don't suppose you have any ideas as to how to prompt her memory?"

"I'm afraid not," he said. "My own grandparents forget my name sometimes, but I don't think any of them has ever forgotten… what is it she's supposed to have done?"

"Murdered Linnea's mother." I was doing a *really* good job at sticking to date-appropriate topics.

His brows shot up. "That seems unlikely. I know your grandmother's not exactly been known for being straight with you… not to be rude."

"No, she really hasn't." I gave an eye roll. "I don't think she murdered anyone, but I definitely think she knows more than she's letting on. At this rate, the Wardens might have better luck getting to the truth."

"You think they might be able to find out?"

"They might," I admitted, "but the one thing they can't do is help with Aunt Shannon. We can't tell them about her challenge to my leadership. I don't know how widely word has already spread. Have you heard anything?"

"No, but I only hear gossip about Sky Hopper players." He leaned back in his seat as our drinks appeared on the table. "Does that mean the Wardens won't come to Wildwood Heath?"

"I doubt Ramsey would allow it," I said. "Though leaving town might be tricky. I wouldn't be surprised if my aunt was keeping tabs and waiting for another excuse to get up to mischief while I'm not around."

"I'm sure your brother will account for that when he contacts them," he said. "How about your dad? What did he suggest?"

"Dad's been great," I replied. "We didn't really talk about the Wardens, but… well, Rowan had the idea of calling a certain pair of reporters and asking them to find something that'll turn my aunt's supporters against her. Something truly scandalous."

He arched a brow. "Would they be able to do that?"

"Absolutely, but nobody else in the family wants the reporters snooping around. Including me. If they find out about Mum…"

"You mean Clarice and Speck, right?" he said. "Didn't they stop working for that tabloid?"

"Yes, but I don't trust them." That was an understatement, really. "If they're really switching to sports journalism, you might run into them on the road."

"I might." He'd recently given me the news that the Sky Hopper team he captained had qualified to compete on a national level, but if the team accepted the offer, they'd be invited to a preliminary match and then potentially be sent on a tour of the country by the year's end. It was his lifelong dream, and I was thrilled for him, but going with him would be out of the question as long as I remained Head Witch.

When a long pause ensued, I decided to push ahead with the inevitable question. "When do you have to decide if you're entering the preliminaries for next year's championships?"

"Ah… by next week," he said apologetically. "I know it's pretty short notice."

"You have to say yes," I insisted. "Don't let my situation deter you."

"I don't want to be gone when you're dealing with so much crap back home."

My heart twisted, but I forced the emotions off my face. "It's fine. You won't be gone forever."

Undeniably, losing one of my main supporters would make it even harder to deal with the next obstacle the universe threw at me, whether it involved my aunt or the demons, but this wasn't about me.

He reached out and took my hand again. "I'll always be a phone call away. Anytime you need me, I'll be there."

I managed a smile. "I appreciate that."

After my date with Harvey, I headed home. As much as I'd wanted to go back to his place instead, he had sports practise at some ungodly hour the following morning to make sure the team was as prepared as possible for the upcoming preliminary match. I was a light enough sleeper that I resignedly agreed with his offer to walk me home instead, and he kissed me so hard on the doorstep that my toes curled.

I had expected Ramsey to stay at his office overnight, so it came as a surprise when I entered the house and found my brother pacing around the kitchen in the semidarkness.

"Robin." He swivelled towards me. "I've set up a meeting with the Wardens."

"Already?" I halted in the doorway. "That was fast."

"I kept calling until I found a group that was available," he said. "You'll meet the team first thing tomorrow morning."

"You said yes on my behalf, did you?" He might have at least asked me first. "Won't Aunt Shannon know if I leave town?"

"She won't guess where you are," he said. "Besides, it's not as if the Head Witch can't go on errands over the weekend."

"I thought she might take advantage of me being gone."

"That's a given anyway. She can't take away your sceptre, remember? There's a limit to what she can do."

He wasn't wrong. And while part of me was irked at him for going behind my back, I was also acutely aware of the ticking clock over my head and that this meeting with the Wardens would be the first step on the road to getting the sceptre out of my hands and the demons back into the deeper afterworld, where they belonged. "All right, then."

If the Wardens could help us hunt down the demon, it ought to be worth the risk of letting my aunt get up to more mischief while I was out of town. Right?

4

I'd hoped for a good night's sleep, but Tansy woke me up by dropping a piece of birdseed onto my head.

"Don't sleep in." She dropped another seed on my nose. "This is our chance to meet the Wardens and send a team of monster hunters after those demons."

I yawned. "I wouldn't count on it. Ramsey didn't say for sure that they could help, and I got the impression he didn't give them too many details over the phone."

Not that I blamed him. After Linnea's betrayal, asking for help from another group of outsiders was a hell of a risk, but we were short on other options.

Tansy jumped onto my bed frame, her fluffy tail tickling my nose. "They're monster-fighting experts, aren't they?"

"Yes, but I don't know that they specialise in demons the way the Reapers do," I pointed out. "Also, what's more powerful than the sceptre?"

"I'm not the expert." She tickled my nose with her tail again, making me sneeze. "Come on, get up. The quicker we get out of town, the less likely it is that your aunt will notice we're gone."

"Oh, she'll be watching." Of that I had no doubt. "That magpie of hers is probably lurking outside the house right now."

"She isn't. I chased her off." Tansy gave me a final nudge. "C'mon."

I groaned. My familiar was far more of a morning person than I was, and I hadn't caught up on all the sleep I'd lost while stressing out about the trial. Though I had to admit that now was probably the best time to take a clandestine trip to meet with a bunch of monster hunters.

Frankly, I'd rather have met with the monsters themselves than with Aunt Shannon and the rest of the council. As a bonus, this meeting would stop me doing anything unwise like calling a certain pair of reporters to ask for dirt on my aunt. Which was, no doubt, the point.

I went downstairs to find breakfast prepared for the two of us, courtesy of the family chef. I thanked Kimberly for her attentiveness and set about loading my plate with bacon and eggs. Typically, Ramsey had opted for plain toast and seemed more interested in skimming the local newspaper than in the delicious food.

"Who are the Wardens we're meeting with?" I asked him. "Are they local?"

He didn't look up from the paper. "Not exactly."

"What do you mean, not exactly?" I sipped my coffee. "I thought you were calling the local branch. The ones who arrested Linnea."

"They weren't available on such short notice." He put the paper aside. "I called several others, and this group was the first to respond, since they're passing through the area on the way back from another job."

"On the way back to where?"

"Northumberland."

"That's hundreds of miles up north." I frowned at him.

"Wait, do they even know about the Wildwood family? Did you just call all the regional Warden offices, regardless of whether they were located in the same county as us?"

"The local branch isn't *that* close to the Wildwood," he pointed out. "The Wardens are widely dispersed across the country, and their missions are typically wide ranging. They don't have to be local."

True enough, but if they weren't familiar with my family or anything related to the situation, we had a hell of a lot of explaining to do. Or not, if my brother wanted to keep certain details quiet. Did they even know that one of their fellow Warden teams had had to arrest a Reaper?

"Don't look at me like that, Robin," he added. "I did the best I could with the resources I had available. The other teams just didn't have the time to meet us this weekend."

"Too busy hunting rogue vampires?" Tansy hopped onto the table and stole some toast crumbs from my plate.

"Probably." I took another bite of toast. "Ramsey, I'm not criticising. I'm just figuring out if it's going to be worth risking Aunt Shannon getting up to shenanigans while we're gone. Tansy already had to chase off her familiar today."

"Then she can keep an eye out while we're gone."

"I'm not staying behind," Tansy said indignantly. "Send your own familiar."

"Oh, *I'll* watch her," said Horace, making both of us jump. I hadn't realised Mum's familiar was in the kitchen and not upstairs, pacing the landing.

"Are you sure?" I asked.

"If that magpie comes near me, I'll eat him."

I blinked in surprise at his vehemence, which wasn't typical of Mum's familiar. Then again, his witch was in a coma, and her sister had tried to steal her title while she was unconscious. I understood why he'd be as bristly as Prickles the hedgehog. "Maybe don't go that far."

"I'll put my own familiar in charge of watching the coven headquarters," Ramsey said. "Nobody should be in there today, but just in case."

"Good call." I took another mouthful of bacon. "Wait. If the Wardens aren't coming here to Wildwood Heath, where are we meeting them?"

———

"The middle of nowhere" turned out to be the answer. The Wardens had been staying at an inn called the Stables, which was halfway down a country road somewhere north of the Wildwood and isolated enough that my phone signal cut out as soon as we landed via transportation spell.

At least in such a remote location, my sceptre was less likely to draw attention. I hadn't *wanted* to bring it with me, but Ramsey had insisted on me protecting myself. To my surprise, there wasn't a soul on the road aside from us. Where were the Wardens?

"This is the place?" Tansy flicked her tail towards the sole building within sight. "That's a pub, not a stable."

"So it is." I walked closer, seeing that there was indeed a sign saying "The Stables" hanging above the pub door. "Are you sure we've got the right place?"

"I'm sure." Ramsey pushed open the door and walked into the pub on the other side.

A sign hanging over the bar saying "reception" suggested its dual purpose as an inn for travellers, beneath which a greasy-looking man who might have been part troll watched us enter. This had to be a paranormal-run establishment, which would answer the question as to why a group of monster hunters had gone unremarked upon.

There were few patrons drinking at this hour, but a table in the far corner was occupied by a group of the most mismatched individuals I'd ever set eyes on. First was a tall man with long dark hair, who rose upright when he saw us enter, moving with the sort of casual elegance that I might have expected of a vampire if there hadn't been one already sitting next to him. The sulky-looking pale man sipping from a glass of dark-red liquid couldn't be anything other than the undead, but the broad red-haired man on his right was definitely a shifter—another oddity, because werewolves and vampires usually got along about as well as the Wildwoods and the Henbane Coven. On the werewolf's other side sat an athletic-looking woman with her dark hair swept back in a bun. She leaned forward in her seat to watch our approach. A second woman—a witch, I assumed—eyed my sceptre warily from her seat next to the vampire.

"Is that them?" Tansy whispered in my ear. "Two witches, a vampire, a werewolf, and… what's that other guy?"

"Quiet," I whispered. "They might be able to understand you."

"I doubt it," she muttered back. "He smells nice."

"Tansy."

Without remarking on my familiar's comment, the elegant man extended a hand to shake Ramsey's. "I'm Tam. We spoke on the phone."

"We did," Ramsey agreed. "I'm Ramsey ,and this is my sister, Robin. You told me that your team had had experience in dealing with demons and that you were on your way back from a case."

"That's right." Tam shook my hand next. "You must be Robin."

"I am." His hand was cool but not the icy cold I'd expected of a vampire. "Nice to meet you. This is Tansy, my familiar."

Tansy squeaked a greeting that nobody at the table understood, evidenced by their blank expressions. She followed it up by whispering "I told you so" in my ear.

"Please sit down." Tam gestured to two unoccupied chairs that had already been laid out for us. "This is my team."

The werewolf leaned over to shake Ramsey's hand then mine. "Hey. I'm Callum."

"Perry." The athletic-looking woman shook our hands next. "Your familiar's adorable."

"Why, thank you." Tansy jumped onto the table and preened, showing off her fluffy tail.

"Don't let it go to your head," I told her.

The other witch gave a shy smile but didn't offer to shake my hand. "I'm Farley."

She nudged the pale man at her side until he muttered, "I'm Maurice."

Definitely a vampire. He'd spoken with a Yorkshire accent, which wasn't what I'd expected of a vampire, but I hadn't met that many. He also didn't look old by vampire standards, but it was hard to tell with the living dead.

"Now the introductions are out of the way," said Ramsey with a hint of impatience, "I'd like you to help us track down some demons. I'm told you have experience in that area?"

"A fair bit," Perry agreed. "We're pretty tuned in to reports of demon incidents, but our latest mission was to hunt a misbehaving goblin, not a demon."

"Sounds like an interesting story." I already had a hundred questions, and zero of them were related to the actual reason we'd wanted to meet with them, but when Ramsey gave me a pointed look, I suppressed my curiosity.

"You said you'd give us more information than you offered on the phone when we met in person," Tam said to my brother. "A demon is possessing someone from your town, is that right?"

"That's right," Ramsey said. "A few weeks ago, a local witch was possessed and then left town. If she's still alive, she's lying low."

"I can't imagine the demon would have left her alive," Perry remarked. "Did she summon it?"

"With help," I replied. "They made some kind of deal."

We hadn't discussed how much to share of the incident with Leona. Ramsey had made it clear that I wasn't to mention our mother's comatose state, but it'd be tricky to discuss the demons without mentioning how my grandmother had been the one to kick off their grudge in the first place.

"You want to find them before they find you?" Callum asked. "Do I have that right?"

"Pretty much." I glanced at Ramsey. "The demon… kind of has a personal grudge against our family."

"Ouch." Perry winced. "How'd you manage that?"

I shrugged. "Bad luck. How do you normally deal with demons, then? You don't have powers like the Reapers do."

Come to think of it, vampires couldn't be possessed. Maybe that was why this group had one on their team, but the guy seemed a little antisocial to say the least.

"No, but we have ways of dealing with them," Tam said. "Anything we can't handle, we call in the Reapers, but we haven't had to do that yet."

Hmm. Did they know of Linnea's betrayal? If they weren't local, they might not, but the subject was bound to come up if they thought of the Reapers as a potential backup option.

"Sage is your best friend," said Perry. "Though I've heard that sceptre of yours is powerful enough to banish a demon single-handedly without backup."

All eyes turned towards the long instrument with its inset purple gem, which I'd leaned against my chair in the manner that so irked my grandmother. My brother's jaw tensed, and I could almost hear his unspoken instruction not to give anything away as if he was telepathically beaming his thoughts directly into my brain.

"Not without backup," I said carefully. "It depends on… on how strong the demon is."

"The ones you're dealing with are class three, right?" Perry went on. "I can see where that'd be trickier than a class one or two but not impossible."

"Not if the demon isn't alone."

Ramsey's heel pressed into the side of my ankle, but I edged my foot away. How was I supposed to ask for their help without giving any details of the sticky situation we'd ended up mired in?

Perry raised a brow. "What, more than one demon?"

"And monsters from the afterworld too," I added. "Like I said, they have a real grudge against my family."

"They?" Tam echoed. "More than one demon… working together?"

"Two of them." I moved my leg further from Ramsey. "That's why we ideally need to find Leona—she's the witch who got possessed—before the other demon manages to get out of the afterworld again."

"They're tag-teaming?" Perry gave a low whistle. "I can see why you wanted our help. Whereabouts was this Leona person last seen?"

"Her whereabouts are unknown, as we discussed on the phone," Ramsey cut in. "In the event that the original summoner survived, I sent a photo of her so that you can ask the locals if they've seen anyone who matches that description."

"You have a photo of Leona?" I supposed it shouldn't surprise me that he did. "What locals? If we don't know where she is…"

"We'll follow the trail of any recent demon sightings," Perry said. "Though if you think this Leona survived possession, she must be a powerful witch."

"No, she's a magical dud," I replied. "That was part of

their deal. She got the demon's powers, and he got a willing host."

Ramsey pressed the heel of his foot lightly onto my toes. "Also, we need to know what other contacts you have in the area."

"You mean with the local Wardens?" Perry asked. "Sure, Tam has their number."

"We've spoken," he confirmed. "I called them shortly after our call yesterday."

"Then…" I glanced at Ramsey. "Did they tell you about their recent arrest?"

"Yes, they told me about the rogue Reaper." Tam spoke casually, but the rest of the team reacted with barely concealed shock. Farley nearly fell out of her seat, Callum's jaw dropped, and Perry's composure slipped.

"Excuse me?"

Maurice, who kept sipping from his glass of red liquid, was the only team member not to react. "Rogue Reapers are a thing. Same as rogue witches or…"

"Vampires?" said Perry, and he scowled. "I know they're a thing, but they're also astronomically rare. You weren't going to mention that sooner, Tam?"

Ramsey looked as if he regretted this entire endeavour. "Nobody should be discussing a confidential matter in public."

"My apologies," Tam said smoothly. "As you brought up the subject yourself, I assumed it was safe to discuss."

"My brother is being overly cautious." I gave him a nudge with my elbow. "He *did* bring it up, because it's a problem. A Reaper betrayed their own and allied with the demons against our family."

"That's all you need to know," Ramsey interjected. "I won't discuss the matter any further unless it's relevant."

"All right." Perry exchanged raised eyebrows with her

teammates. "You can't expect us not to ask questions, though. Don't Reapers hunt demons for a living?"

"Not sure 'living' is the right word," Callum said with a shudder. "But… yes, they do."

"Yes, and she was arrested by the Wardens," said Ramsey. "What else did they tell you?"

"She's been transferred to another branch," said Tam. "Since our team wasn't involved, the head of the local Wardens didn't give me any more information about where they sent her."

"As far away as possible, I hope." I hoped they'd secured the stone she'd given me by which I could summon her to my side too. That was an artefact that should have belonged to the Reapers, but she must have stolen it when she'd ditched her apprenticeship and murdered her mentor.

"Someone really doesn't like your family," Farley said. "The Wildwoods… I've heard the name."

"I haven't," Callum said.

"Nobody cares," said Maurice.

"Harsh," Callum said lightly. "I *do* know of the Head Witches. Are you really…?"

"Yes." I felt my face heat up as all eyes turned once again to the sceptre. "When I took over as Head Witch, I inherited my predecessor's enemies. Hence the demons. The last time we asked outsiders for help, it didn't work out in our favour, which is why my brother's looking at you as if you're potential bank robbers."

"Well, there's no danger of us betraying you, because we have no idea who you are," Perry said. "Except that you seem to have luck as bad as I do, and that's saying a lot."

I sensed another story there… or several. "Just as long as you can help us find Leona. Or the demon if it killed her and possessed someone else."

"Sure, we can do that," said Perry. "The local Wardens will

be able to point us in the right direction if we need them to, right, Tam?"

"We can pay them a visit," Tam agreed. "And see if they'll share more about that rogue Reaper in person. What else did you want to know?"

"Nothing," Ramsey said through gritted teeth.

"I'd like to know what led the Reaper to turn to the demons for help." This time, Ramsey's foot came down on my toes, hard, and I bit back a wince.

"That won't be necessary," he said. "I'll call the local branch myself and see if they'll talk directly to me."

"I thought you were focused on Leona." I rubbed my foot. He'd asked for these people's help, hadn't he? The Wardens had almost as many contacts as the Reapers did, and with less of the reluctance to actually share any of that information with the rest of us mere mortals. Why shouldn't they use those contacts to find out what had driven Linnea to the dark side?

"What's the Reaper's name?" asked Perry, looking between the pair of us curiously. "I bet she's in our records."

I blinked. "You have Reapers in your records?"

"No, but she wasn't always a Reaper, was she?" Perry nodded to Tam. "Reapers aren't allowed to have children, so her mother can't have been one either."

"I forgot that," Callum said. "Seems harsh."

"It does," Perry agreed. "I thought the Wardens were sticklers for the rules, but I'm surprised the Reapers don't get stabbed in the back more often. Or scythed in the back, as it were."

I was starting to like her more and more the longer we spoke. The others, I was less sure about. Callum seemed friendly enough, and Farley was more reserved, while I didn't know what to make of Tam. He'd spoken with a faint northern accent but not strong enough for him to belong to a specific region, and I couldn't figure out what kind of para-normal he was.

As for Maurice, he acted like he'd been forced here under duress. Which might be true, given that vampires didn't usually work for the monster hunters. They were more likely to be amongst the misbehaving beasties who needed to be hunted down, in fact. I'd still rather have spent the day with an antisocial vampire than with my aunt, but could I rely on these people to help me achieve the impossible and banish the demons permanently?

"The Reaper's name is Linnea," I told Tam. "Linnea… what's her surname, Ramsey?"

"I have no idea," he grated out. "I doubt you'll find out either. The Reapers keep their secrets under lock and key."

"We'll do some more poking around," Perry offered. "We're in the area for a bit. Might as well make ourselves useful."

"Is that all?" Tam asked my brother. "We'll put out feelers in the area to find the demon and pay the local Wardens' branch a visit to see if they've heard of any similar incidents. Anything else?"

"No, that will do," Ramsey said crisply. "Call my office if you learn anything of note."

He rose to his feet and gestured for me to do the same. I ignored him and smiled at the others. "Thanks for the help. It's appreciated."

"Anytime." Perry grinned back and gave Tansy a stroke when my familiar jumped onto the table to show off her fluffy tail to everyone again. "Nice meeting you both."

I was pretty sure she meant me and Tansy, not me and my brother, and from his scowl, he knew it too. Picking up my sceptre, I waved goodbye to the Wardens before following my brother out of the pub.

Tansy scampered at my side. "I like them."

"They called you adorable. Of course you do."

She poked her tongue out at me. "I don't think they're going to betray you either."

"You can't know that," Ramsey said sternly. "Nor you, Robin."

"I have good instincts," Tansy said. "They seem odd but genuine. Most of them don't know who the Wildwoods are. They aren't going to call the press."

"Isn't that one of the reasons you picked them?" I asked my brother. "They're used to taking part in confidential missions."

He grunted. "That doesn't mean we need our coven's history exposed to strangers."

"If you tell them not to talk, they won't." The vampire might… and now I thought about it, couldn't he read minds? *Uh-oh.* If he'd looked into my thoughts at any moment during our conversation, all the effort that I'd made to avoid mentioning Mum or Grandma had been in vain. But the others hadn't mentioned it as a potential problem, nor did they seem concerned that he'd eavesdrop on their own secrets either.

"They still might take advantage of knowing such incriminating information about a Head Witch," he said. "We'll take their help finding the demon and part ways if they're unable to track Leona within the week."

"We need their help. You know that," I said. "Maybe they *can* find out why Linnea hates us so much. What's the problem with doing a little research?"

"That would lead them to find out we have a former Head Witch accused of a crime, no current functioning coven leader, and a leadership crisis."

"Not necessarily." He hadn't brought up the vampire's mind-reading ability, but perhaps he'd forgotten, since there weren't any local vampires to Wildwood Heath, and even my all-knowing brother had some weak spots. *Best keep that quiet, then.* "I don't think they're likely to take advantage of us. If you thought that, you wouldn't have called them in the first place, would you?"

"There were few options." He turned away from the pub and down the country lane. "You can't be too careful, Robin. You have enemies out there."

"Not much out there but sheep." Tansy gestured to the surrounding fields. "Lighten up. What's the alternative, send Robin to fight Leona alone?"

"I'm not cool with that," I added. "I'd say we can trust them."

"And I say we'll reserve judgement either way until they've proven they can find the demon," Ramsey retorted, and I knew from his tone that there'd be no arguing with that one. "Now, let's get back to Wildwood Heath before anyone notices the Head Witch is gone."

5

When we got back home, we found Mum's familiar lurking near the back garden fence with a feather sticking out of his mouth.

"You didn't actually eat her, did you?" I asked. "Myrtle, I mean."

"No. I just scared her a little," said Horace. "I hope your trip out of town was worth the risk."

"It was." I gave Ramsey a pointed look. "I think the Wardens will be a real help. Ah… how is…?"

"Your mother? No change."

I'd known, of course, but I always asked anyway. My phone signal had come back, revealing that Piper had texted me several times since I'd left. I replied, asking if she wanted to go and hang out somewhere that preferably wasn't my mother's house. I hadn't properly updated her on the details of the trial, since I'd already had so many people to check in with the previous day, and she'd been temporarily taken off gardening duty courtesy of Mum's overzealous familiar. You'd have thought Mum would have wanted someone to keep her flowerbeds in top shape while she was in a coma, really.

"Where are you going?" Ramsey asked when I made for the front door.

"I'm meeting Piper," I replied. "What's the problem?"

"You don't think you should be practising with the sceptre?" he asked. "If the Wardens do manage to find Leona's location, that might give her incentive to come back and hunt you down."

My heart sank. "I'm not going to be ready either way. You know that."

I'd spent weeks using the sceptre to practise magic, but I was stymied by the fact that I couldn't test out banishment spells on a genuine monster from the afterworld, for obvious reasons. The other issue was that Leona might bring half the afterworld with her when she attacked, which would be too much for even the sceptre to handle.

"That's no reason not to try," he said. "It might save your life."

"Fine." Sighing inwardly, I sent Piper another text and asked if she wanted to meet me in the forest. If I had to spend my free day on tedious magical practise, I might as well have some moral support.

Piper met me five minutes later at the entrance to the Wildwood. Even when she wasn't gardening, her clothes were stained with old mud, and she wore a pair of equally mud-stained boots.

"Sorry Ramsey gave you the boot," I said. "He's the reason I'm out here too. He thinks I ought to be prepared for Leona's inevitable return."

"He thinks she's still alive?" Piper raised a brow. "The demon already finished her off, surely."

"They did make a deal."

"Even if she *is* alive, she won't be able to get past the sage barrier, will she?" She gestured to the surrounding trees and the thick undergrowth, which hid the barrier of sage that had been placed around the entire town. Sage repelled all spirits, ghost and demon alike, and it'd become part of the local police's new routine to check the sage barrier daily and replace any that had been washed away by the rain. Dad, for his part, made sure the shifters' part of town remained protected too.

"No, but you know what my brother's like." I lifted the sceptre. "I thought I'd humour him and practise some combat spells."

"That's why I wore these clothes." She gestured to her muddy boots. "If you have to throw someone around the forest, it might as well be me. I have nothing else to do today."

We found a deserted clearing to practise in. I told her about our meeting with the Wardens while we ran through every spell that might work against demons or other afterworld monsters. Since the sceptre was basically a high-powered wand, the spellcasting itself wasn't the problem, but the fact that it nearly came up to my shoulder and was hard to swing around in complicated motions without causing myself injury created a challenge. Luckily, Piper didn't laugh at the many times I tripped over or overbalanced, and I was pretty sure I could count on one hand the number of people who'd had enough trust in me to let me use them for target practise too. Luckily, the worst I did was accidentally transport her up a tree—much to the annoyance of Tansy, who'd been stalking a pigeon in the tree in question.

"Do you want to practise on me for a change?" I asked Piper when she'd climbed down.

"If turning a demon into a petunia was possible, that'd be right up my alley," she said. "As it is, I'm fine with being a guinea pig instead."

"If you're sure."

She was a good cheerleader, even when I screwed up, and I had to admit it was nice to pretend for a while that I had some semblance of control over my ability to fight off the demon.

When we were done with practising, I went to the café to hang out with Rowan for a relaxing afternoon playing video games. Then I spent Sunday at Dad's house with Jessica and the kids. It was a welcome change from the stress of the previous week, but as much as I wished the weekend would last forever, I soon found myself facing down the barrel of Monday morning.

Specifically, the part when I had to face the council again.

I arrived at the office to a new mountain of admin that had accumulated over the weekend. Chloe and I joined forces to sort out the backlog while I told her all about my visit to the Wardens with Ramsey. I'd thought Grandma might show up and lecture me on sharing her secrets with the Wardens, but she didn't. Whatever Ramsey claimed, she *was* avoiding me, and my questions concerning her role in Linnea's betrayal multiplied by the hour.

Not that I had much time to dwell on that. Before long, it was time to face whatever Aunt Shannon had cooked up in the past couple of days. The meeting was set for eleven that morning, but when I opened the door, nobody else was inside. It was unusual for me to be the first person there, but they could hardly accuse me of shirking my duty again.

I sat down and waited. And waited.

"What's taking so long?" I checked the time, as I'd done every thirty seconds since I'd come in. Ten minutes had elapsed. Too long to be coincidental. I'd been certain that Aunt Shannon would have taken full advantage of my absence over the weekend and dug out some new obscure rule with which to bludgeon me, but she was nowhere to be seen.

Unfortunately, neither was anyone else.

"I'll go and check on them," Chloe offered. "They might have forgotten the meeting time."

I had my doubts. This had my aunt's name written all over it. I remained seated, though, waiting for Chloe's return. Given the quietness inside the building, it came as no surprise when she returned in less than a minute, announcing that none of the council members was in the coven headquarters.

"They're not in the building at all?" I asked. "Including Aunt Shannon?"

"Her office door was locked," she said. "I didn't hear a sound, though. There are a few people upstairs, but none of the council members are here."

Seriously? "Has she asked them all to go on strike?"

"Maybe," she said. "Belinda should be here, though. She's on your side."

"She should be." My hands clenched. "What did my aunt do this time?"

"We can get on with some other work while the others are gone," she suggested. "There's still that admin backlog."

"Because that's more important than finding the demon?"

"Didn't you say the Wardens were looking for Leona?"

"I did." The entire council disappearing was not an issue I could ignore, however. "We haven't heard back from them yet, but I can't let Aunt Shannon steal the entire council away whenever she feels like it."

Really, it was a pity I couldn't set the Wardens on *her*.

Chloe's brow furrowed. "I suppose while you were out of town, she might have contacted the council, but you weren't gone for long, were you?"

"No. My brother set the meeting for stupid o'clock on

Saturday morning to avoid exactly this." I rose to my feet. "I'm sure this'll end up being my fault, though he's the one who called them in the first place."

Grandma popped out of thin air. "Your brother called *whom?*"

"The Wardens." I took a startled step back. "Have you been listening to us all along?"

I'd suspected as much, but she rarely ventured outside of the office except to go back to the house and watch Mum. She certainly didn't come to meetings.

"And why exactly did he call them?" she asked.

"They're going to help us find the missing demon that possessed Leona and banish it."

"They're outsiders!" she objected. "They're not supposed to be involved in coven business."

"I didn't tell them about Mum. Or you. Or anything about being Head Witch at all, really."

"I should hope not," she said. "First, the Reapers, and now, this. And you wonder why people keep trying to kill you?"

"I know perfectly well why people are trying to kill me." *Because of you,* I added silently. "They have contacts who can help find the demon before anyone else gets hurt. Also... maybe they can find out what led Linnea to turn against the coven."

I was already braced when a gust of wind swept through the room and knocked over half the chairs.

"You did *what?*" Grandma boomed. "Call them and tell them to cease poking their noses into our business."

"Too late," I said from behind my arms, shielding my face from the sudden onslaught of her poltergeist powers. "We need to know why a Reaper wants us dead, and if you don't remember..."

"It's irrelevant," she shot at me. "The false Reaper is in jail, isn't she?"

"It's the exact opposite of irrelevant." I lowered my arms. "What did you do to her? What did she mean when she claimed our coven killed her mother?"

"A misunderstanding," she said. "I did nothing to her."

"But—" I took a step back when another gust of wind struck the room, and she vanished in the same instant, chairs rattling in her wake. "How can she expect me not to go elsewhere looking for answers if she won't tell me?"

"I don't know." Chloe began straightening up the chairs. "Maybe she really doesn't remember. Ghosts can be touchy about losing their memories."

I had my doubts, but Grandma was as stubborn as any of my family members and had the added advantage of being able to vanish into the afterworld whenever she didn't want to talk to anyone.

When we'd tidied the room, I resigned myself to going back to the office and the mountain of paperwork draped across both my desk and Chloe's. Some was obscure coven documents containing laws we might be able to employ to stop Aunt Shannon's schemes, but the rest was just, well, junk.

"Anything in there about the interim coven leader being allowed to tell the rest of the council to go on strike?" I asked Chloe. "Wouldn't that count as making a major decision?"

"No, it wouldn't, which is probably why she did it," said Chloe, her mouth turning down at the corners. "We might be able to convince them to come back, but it depends on what she told them. And… well. It might be worth spending our time on this instead."

"What, admin?"

"No." She held up a wad of paper that was thicker than my leg. "I'm trying to find a way to challenge her claim to coven leadership outright. I'm sure there's something in here that allows us to unseat an interim coven leader who puts their own interests first."

"Really?" A quick glance confirmed that I'd need her to translate the documents from legal speak into plain English so that I could make sense of them, but if anyone could, it was Chloe. "You mean prove that my aunt was acting against the coven's interests for her own gain? That might actually work?"

"Theoretically, but it's not easy." She laid the papers on her desk. "There's nobody to prove it to. We're the authority ourselves, after all, and she has a lot of allies."

"Who outranks her?" Plenty of people did… but not in this town. "There's the other Head Witches."

"Your mother wouldn't want us telling the others that she's in a coma. Some might take advantage."

"I know." My hands curled into fists. "It isn't right that Aunt Shannon has this much power, even temporarily. Look at those illegal potions she was selling. Her misuse of the coven's funds. And more that I probably don't know about. Aren't those all good enough reasons to oust her?"

I looked at my phone, tempted once again to call the number I'd saved and ask the reporters to see what other dirty secrets they could unearth.

"If her supporters don't care about any of that, there's not much we can do," she said. "Also, the other Head Witches… there's limits to whether they can get involved in other covens' disputes."

"This isn't just a coven dispute. She wants to take my sceptre." My hands itched to make the call, but I'd told my brother I wouldn't, and I intended to keep my word until I had no choice. Or at least until we next heard from the Wardens.

"Is there anything else you want to do?" she asked. "We

can see where the council members are. I have their numbers."

"Or we can drop by their houses," I said. "And there's one house that's closer than the rest."

Yes, I knew paying my aunt a house call would end badly, but I wanted to know how she'd managed to get even Belinda to stay at home from the office. Besides, I was a little concerned she'd invited the council to her house for a meeting instead and that they were cooking up some new scheme to undermine me.

"Are you sure?" Chloe said. "She might be trying to set you up."

"She might," I agreed, "but she orchestrated this, and I want to know her reasoning. Also, is there some kind of rule I can invoke to give her a penalty for not coming to work?"

"Not that I know of. Coven leaders can do as they like."

That figured. My aunt was notorious for staying ten steps ahead of me, and calling for an office strike hadn't been on my radar as her next move.

First, I went to the coven's garden to collect my familiar. Tansy, typically, was stalking a pigeon near the hedge maze at the back, and she groaned when my arrival caused it to take off.

"What is it?" she asked.

"We're going to visit Aunt Shannon."

"Isn't she in the meeting room?"

"Nope. She's skiving off, and she convinced the rest of the council to do the same."

I didn't bother keeping my voice down in case a certain magpie was hiding somewhere in the hedge maze. The maze itself had been the site of the initial dispute between our coven and the Henbanes' next door, and from here, I could see that their headquarters looked decidedly derelict behind its overgrown garden.

"I hope Tiffany hasn't found out about all this from in jail," I muttered to Tansy as we walked through the coven headquarters to the front door. "She'll be laughing her head off at the thought of my aunt taking my title."

"Are you sure you're making the right choice by going to her house?"

"No, but it's not a good idea to call the reporters either, and that's what I'll end up doing if I don't check up to see what she's doing. I can't picture her putting her feet up and watching TV, somehow."

Tansy snorted. "No, that's not her style."

My aunt's house was a mirror of its neighbour, its wide-open windows giving the impression that the owner didn't much care that we knew they were at home. With Tansy perched on my shoulder, I rapped on the door with my knuckles.

Aunt Shannon answered, a smile tilting her mouth. "Yes, Robin?"

"You should be at work," I said bluntly. "Is there a reason you skipped today's meeting? I thought the coven leader was supposed to set a good example to the other witches."

"*I* thought you'd be busy meeting with your new friends again."

Of course she knew about our trip to see the Wardens. "The rest of the council is absent too. You don't happen to know anything about that, do you?"

"I assume they came to the conclusion that it's rather pointless to host a coven meeting when there's nothing to discuss," she said. "As the Head Witch is ineffective and the coven leader is unable to act, it seems like a waste of time, doesn't it?"

"I beg to differ," I said. "There's plenty to discuss. Such as the demons."

"I thought your new friends were handling that."

She wasn't spying on our meeting, was she? No, she'd most likely guessed. It wasn't that hard to make the obvious logical leap, and she spoke with certainty in an attempt to rattle me. "You're surely aware that it's my duty as Head Witch to keep the council informed of any developments. It's somewhat difficult to do that when nobody shows up."

"Ah, but you're known to disappear at times of crisis, so they have no reason to expect you to inform them of anything."

My brief attempt at diplomacy flew headfirst out the window. "What did you do to convince Belinda not to show up, out of curiosity?"

"Nothing whatsoever," she said benignly. "I expect that she lost faith in you, like the others… and that will likely not improve when they learn the truth that you have yet to divulge, concerning the demons' link to your predecessor."

I should have seen that one coming. In truth, I was impressed that I'd managed to get this far without the rest of the council learning all the details about why Grandma had ticked them off.

"That's more Grandma's history than mine," I told her. "If you want to admit that Mum ended up in a coma because of the last Head Witch and undermine their faith in her as well, that won't work out in anyone's favour, including yours."

"I don't need them to respect the last Head Witch. They've seen for themselves that she's nothing more than an angry spirit trapped in this realm beyond her time."

My mouth fell open. Was she seriously insulting *Grandma* now? "They worked with Grandma for years. They respect her. More than you, I'm betting."

But what if she was right? As I knew all too well, Grandma's recent behaviour was so erratic that nobody could rely on her to do anything except knock the furniture around.

Aunt Shannon didn't even blink. "They certainly have no reason to believe you can handle the demons."

"And you?" I queried. "I might remind you that *I've* never been possessed. You'll have a hard time convincing them of your competence after the last time."

Her smile returned, though it was more strained than before. "I'm sure everyone is looking forward to your masterful display of your powers against the demons. Should you fail, I'll be ready."

"The sceptre won't choose you." *Even if I'm dead. I hope.*

"We'll see." She closed the door without another word. I might have persisted, but what would have been the point? I'd only succeeded in winding myself up even further, as evidenced by the flock of pigeons circling overhead when I turned away from the house.

"I hope they leave a mess all over her roof," Tansy said. "She's asking for someone to put acorns inside her pillowcase."

"Please don't." I rubbed my forehead. "I don't know why I thought talking to her would be of any use."

I was halfway to the coven headquarters when Chloe came running out the door. "I called Belinda, and she claims a message went out from the office informing the council they didn't have to come in."

"A phone message?" Had my aunt been tampering with the landlines at headquarters now?

"I think so," she said. "I don't know how she did it."

"She also insulted the former Head Witch," I said. "Nothing she does surprises me anymore. Should we check she didn't put any more spells on the phone lines?"

"That's probably a good idea." Worry clouded her eyes. "I really thought winning an extra month would…"

"Put her feud on hold?" I shook my head. "No. It's just escalated. This is war."

6

It took an hour for Chloe and me to find the office phone that my aunt had enchanted to send out an automated call and unravel the complex magic binding it. Someone had been busy over the weekend.

"You have to hand it to her for persistence," I said when the spell finally unravelled like a knitted blanket. "I hope that's the only phone she enchanted."

Knowing her, she might have sent out emails, too, but since none of the other council members owned a computer, they'd have been considerably less effective.

"Would you like me to call everyone and ask them to come in this afternoon?" asked Chloe. "Belinda was very apologetic on the phone. I think she'll be willing to listen."

"I might as well pay her a house visit," I said. "To see what Aunt Shannon actually told her. I assume she didn't give the details of Grandma's feud with the demons."

"I don't think so," Chloe said. "Belinda might be able to shed some light on what she did to convince the others to join her team too."

"Blackmail, I told you," Tansy said from the desk. "Are you going to see her now?"

I checked the time. "We can drop in at Belinda's house before lunch, can't we?"

Chloe nodded. "She doesn't live too far from here. I'll give you her address."

With Tansy at my side, I followed Chloe's directions down the street to a cul-de-sac lined with detached bungalows that backed onto the Wildwood. I knocked on the door.

Belinda answered with a large pile of knitting in her arms. "Head Witch."

"That's me." She didn't have to call me by my title and not my name, but I guessed old habits were hard to break. "If it's all right, can I come in?"

"Of course." She shuffled backwards into a living room filled with more knitting than could possibly belong to one person. "My husband's outside."

I'd already assumed as much by the loud masculine out-of-tune singing drifting through the open window. "I understand you received a message saying you didn't need to come in to work?"

She sat down in an armchair and began knitting again. "Yes, the message said there was no need to, as there was… ah. No active Head Witch."

Ouch. "Did it have her name attached? Ah, Shannon Wildwood's, I mean?"

"You assumed correctly," she said. "The interim coven leader still claims authority in such matters."

"That figures." I tried unsuccessfully to clamp down my annoyance. "If it's not inappropriate for me to ask, I wondered why Janine decided to take her side. According to my grandmother—the former Head Witch—she and Shannon Wildwood have never been allies before."

"Your grandmother." Her eyes widened a fraction. "You're still consulting with her?"

"I am." No need to let on how strained our relationship was. "My grandmother has been helping me as Head Witch for some time and has no intention of supporting a new one."

"No, I suppose she wouldn't," said Belinda. "Janine… it does seem odd, but I suppose Shannon put a compelling case together."

"She broke the law." I didn't see any more point in dancing around the subject. "Does nobody else recall the incident with the illegal potions only a few months ago?"

Belinda flushed. "*I* remember, but it's possible the others were… ah, persuaded to forget."

Bribery. Tansy had been right.

"I'd like to persuade them to remember." I was pretty sure I'd gone past the point of typical Head Witch propriety, but if I didn't make it clear how much we stood to lose from my aunt's challenge, I ran the risk of her working the same persuasion on my one remaining ally. "Not least because we have a crisis to deal with, and I'll need the support of the entire council in the event of another attack from the demons."

Finally, she looked up from her knitting. "Is that likely?"

"Leona is still at large." That much everyone was aware of. "If she's alive, she'll be out for revenge, and so will the demon possessing her. The recent attack proved we have other enemies too."

"That is true." She resumed her knitting. "Your aunt gave the impression that the matter was in her hands."

"She has no plan," I said bluntly. "She hasn't thought of anything past her desire to claim the sceptre. All of you must know she's in this for her own gain. She took advantage of what happened to my mother without a thought to what might happen if another similar threat arrives."

Her knitting stilled. "I thought so. Shannon… she paid me a visit shortly before the recent attack."

Before Linnea's betrayal? "What did she say?"

"That she had reason to believe there wouldn't be a Head Witch for much longer and that she needed the support of the council in the event that the coven leader was also incapacitated."

"She knew?" Impossible. She *couldn't* have. Was she psychic now?

"That I can't say, Head Witch." She lowered her knitting needles. "I would assume she also visited the others and that she told them this as well as making… *references* to certain matters they'd have preferred to keep quiet. I'm sure you understand what I mean."

"Blackmail." No point in being discreet. "But she had nothing on you."

"No." She put her knitting aside. "She didn't. Would you like me to return to the office today?"

"Not yet," I said. "I think I'll have a word with the others."

"I wouldn't advise it," she said gravely. "Shannon knows all of us inside and out. She's not going to easily lose support unless someone with a higher rank brings a case against her that's equally compelling."

Another Head Witch. That was what it came down to. Or my mother, if she woke up, but that wasn't the point. How could my aunt have foreseen Linnea's betrayal? Did she have access to a crystal ball that I wasn't aware of?

"You'd think more people would remember her history," I said.

"You'll be surprised," she murmured. "She covers her tracks well. Good luck, Robin."

I left the room full of knitting behind and met my familiar outside. Judging by the black and white feathers scattered on the lawn, she'd been busy.

"Did those feathers come from Aunt Shannon's familiar?" I guessed.

"She tried to land on the windowsill," said Tansy. "I persuaded her otherwise."

"Thanks." I blew out a breath. "Any ideas as to how Aunt Shannon knew Mum would end up in a coma?"

"She didn't, did she?"

"Belinda said she went to see the council members *before* the incident with Linnea." I rubbed my forehead. "Did she also visit a Seer?"

"Or borrow the Seeing Stone?" Tansy suggested.

"The visions it shows aren't that specific." Unease trickled down my spine. Was another Head Witch helping her bid for power? "I think we need to give Jemima a call."

Jemima was the one Head Witch who Mum had trusted enough to give me instruction, after all. I made my way back to the office and told Chloe the bad news.

"It's got to be the Seeing Stone," I finished. "That or a crystal ball, but… it seems impossible."

"She can't have the Seeing Stone," said Chloe. "Mavis was the last person to have it, and she's not in the area."

"Maybe she borrowed one from another region." The Seeing Stone was a million times more accurate than any Seer, who tended to have visions of the unhelpful "the bus will be five minutes late" variety. Not important matters that would affect the future of a coven. "I think it's worth calling Mavis, too, then."

"I'll call Jemima first," said Chloe. "Maybe write to some in other regions… but we'll need to be careful how we approach this."

"Mention that someone is using blackmail to try to steal a sceptre," I said. "Belinda all but confirmed that's what Aunt Shannon did to convince them to forget her own dodgy history."

"I *knew* it." Tansy bounced up and down on the spot. "I told you so."

"Except Belinda, because there was nothing she could use against her," I added. "Yes, you were right, Tansy, but what am I supposed to do if this doesn't work?"

"Return the favour?" Tansy suggested.

"What, blackmail her right back?" Was it even possible to out-blackmail the blackmailer? No, playing her game might blow up in my face, and I wouldn't resort to those tactics myself besides. She knew I wouldn't, and that was why she was so confident of winning the vote.

"Find out what she used to blackmail them and stop her from carrying through on whatever threats she made?" Tansy suggested. "Or save yourself the bother and just push your aunt into a pond and let nature sort her out?"

I rolled my eyes. "I think calling the other Head Witches is a good idea."

"I'll come up with a script and call them myself," Chloe said. "Is that okay?"

"Of course." My own phone buzzed in my pocket. *Ramsey.* "I think my brother wants me to come to the police station."

Had he heard from the Wardens already? My heartbeat kicked up. Thanks to my aunt's shenanigans, the reality of their hunt for Leona had slipped to the back of my mind. But if they'd found her…

I wasn't ready, I knew, but with a team of Wardens at my back, the odds were better than before.

"Go and see him," Chloe offered. "I'll call the other Head Witches while you're gone."

"I'll be back later."

It was another sunny day, but the chill in the air indicated summer would soon be on the way out. Not a welcome thought, given that autumn meant Samhain, which would signal my only chance to get the sceptre out of my hands before the year was out. Banishing the demons before then was the only way to make that happen, I knew, yet that didn't mean the thought of facing Leona again didn't fill me with dread. Who knew how many new allies she'd gathered in her long absence?

Tansy and I entered the police station and found Ramsey already waiting for me in the reception area.

"The Wardens called." He beckoned me into his office. "Less than an hour ago."

Straight to business, then. Tansy and I entered the small, neat room where he spent the majority of his time. "And? Don't leave me in suspense."

"They managed to get some information from the local Wardens' branch," he said. "Concerning Linnea."

Linnea? "Like what? Did they find out why she thinks our coven killed her mother?"

"No, but they found out her surname," he said. "Linnea Burdock. It's her coven name too."

"She belonged to a coven?" I guessed that made sense if she'd been a witch before joining the Reapers, but I'd assumed the Wardens would have been making the demon a priority instead.

"Yes, and her mother was coven leader," he said. "Before her death about two decades ago. The circumstances were… murky. It also sounds like the entire coven was disbanded around the same time."

Wait a moment. "Two decades. Isn't that when…?"

"When Robin's grandmother banished the demons?" Tansy put in. "How'd she die?"

"That, I don't know," said Ramsey. "The Wardens didn't either, but Tam said that the higher-ups wouldn't let that information out to anyone outside of their own branch."

"How about we drop by the local Wardens' branch ourselves and see if they'll talk in person?"

"No," he said. "We can't risk you leaving town again."

"Since when?" I blinked. "You were fine with us going to see the Wardens the last time."

"That was before the Wardens started hunting down the demon," he said. "They said they were making progress at tracking down Leona, and once they have the demon's attention, only the sage barrier around the town will stop her from entering Wildwood Heath. If you leave, you'll make yourself vulnerable."

"Then…. I'm stuck here."

"No, you're safe," he corrected.

"Sure I am," I said. "Safe in the same place as my aunt, who turns out to have been conspiring with the council *before* Mum fell into a coma. I'm pretty sure she has access to a Seeing Stone somehow, because she knew Linnea would betray us and that Mum would be taken out of action."

"Who told you that?"

"Belinda did," I said. "She also confirmed that Aunt Shannon's blackmailing the other council members, and she sent out a message telling everyone not to bother coming to work by putting a spell on the coven's phone lines."

"You shouldn't be discussing this with the other council members," he said. "You certainly shouldn't have been visiting their houses."

"Aunt Shannon is the one blackmailing them." I should have guessed he'd object to that strategy. "Chloe's calling the other Head Witches to see if any of them are willing to back up my claims against her, but if I'm not allowed to visit them in person…"

"You can't bring the other Head Witches into this either."

"Jemima knows Mum. She's safe." I ground my teeth. "You're just going to shoot down all my plans, aren't you? I could tell you that Aunt Shannon put Mum into a coma herself, and you'd tut and tell me it's somehow my fault."

"Don't be ridiculous," he said. "I'm trying to keep you safe. This is a dangerous game you're playing."

"I'm not playing any game that my aunt didn't already start," I said. "We might have an extra month, but it'll go by fast, and I'll need to stop her from digging out some other rule to smite me with in the meantime."

"That's Chloe's job," he said. "Not to call the other Head Witches and jeopardise our security."

"Did you forget it took the combined efforts of me and several other Head Witches to banish those monsters a few weeks ago?" I breathed in and out, my anger sizzling hot. "I *need* help, and it's not a sin to ask for it. You might want to remember that sometimes."

You'd think not wanting me to be killed by demons would be a big enough incentive.

"You need to be careful where you place your trust," he corrected. "Even with the rest of your council members."

"You're not Head Witch." I'd about had enough. "You don't get to make those decisions."

I turned on my heel and left before I said something even less advisable. I knew throwing my title in his face was the height of childish behaviour, but so was his absurd dedication to making my ability to actually do my job as difficult as possible. It wasn't as if I'd called the press… though the idea was now considerably more tempting than it had been earlier.

"He'll have you grounded next," Tansy remarked.

I grunted. "He can try. You don't think he's being reasonable, do you?"

"Absolutely not," she said. "Tell you what, I'll go and see the Wardens myself. He can't stop *me* from leaving."

"They can't understand you. You know that." I halted outside the police station, my gaze travelling over to the café where Rowan worked. "Maybe I should call Clarice and

Speck after all. It's not like he can think any less of me than he already does."

"Do it," Tansy encouraged. "He didn't say you couldn't call someone from outside town, did he?"

"What… you really think I should call them?" I hadn't expected my familiar to jump on board with my impulse so readily.

"Why not?" she said. "They'll be able to dig up your aunt's sordid history without you having to leave Wildwood Heath and endanger yourself. Then, you hand the evidence over to the other Head Witches. Problem solved."

"That's oversimplifying, Tansy."

Deciding to ask Rowan's advice while I was here, I entered the café and found her busy with the lunch shift. I got in line to buy a latte and sandwich while I waited for her to have a spare moment to talk.

"Hey, Robin," she said when she took my order. "How's work?"

"Quiet, thanks to a certain someone who had everyone else stay at home from the office."

"Did she? Why?"

"Because she's an obstructionist," I said. "When you have a minute, can we talk? I'd like to talk more about… you know, your idea."

She nearly dropped the drink she was preparing. "I'll ask someone to cover for me for ten minutes. This I've gotta hear."

I claimed one of the few unoccupied tables—or Tansy did by planting herself on a chair and flicking crumbs at anyone who came near—and nibbled on my sandwich while I waited for Rowan to escape the flood of customers.

When she did, she claimed the seat Tansy had been guarding and leaned over the table eagerly. "You want to call the reporters? What changed your mind?"

"Ramsey." I gave her a summary of the day's events. "Since I'm confined to Wildwood Heath for the time being, calling Clarice and Speck is something I can do without leaving. If they can find a story worse than the illegal potions incident, it might be enough to convince the other Head Witches to come here and back me up. As a bonus, I'll have more allies when Leona shows up again."

"The Wardens are close to finding her?" She drummed her fingers on the table. "Yeah, I see how that would work. Still risky in a dozen ways, but I think you're right."

"I think it's the only way," I said. "Clarice and Speck aren't exactly trustworthy, but we did make an agreement, and I think I can convince them to poke around. If I make it clear that they aren't to let anyone else in on the story or I won't cooperate, they'll fall over themselves to comply."

"They'll be delighted to," Tansy put in.

"Yeah." Rowan bit her lip, perhaps remembering her own interviews with them. "They're relentless, though. The stories the *Blue Moon* printed... they had been following Grandma's every move since before I was born."

"Huh." *Did they cover the demon incident? Or... the incident with Linnea's coven?* Might I be able to unearth more information on that while I was at it? Kill two birds with one stone? "I think that we might need that level of persistence if we want to stop Aunt Shannon."

"Yeah." She drew in a breath. "I know. She's ruthless."

"And psychic, apparently," I added. "She visited the council *before* Mum fell into a coma and dropped some hints that make me wonder if she knew it was coming."

"She can't have." Rowan glanced back at the counter, where one of her coworkers was gesturing for her to come and help. "She's no Seer."

"I thought not, too, but it's a hell of a coincidence." I

drank the rest of my coffee and stood up. "You'd better get back to work."

"You're calling them now?"

"Might have to go outside." The low-level noise in the café would interfere, and I didn't want anyone to listen in on the call. "I'll do it before I change my mind." Or came to my senses. Whatever worked.

"Go on." She nudged me. "Do it."

While she returned to work, I left the café and scrolled through my list of phone contacts. Clarice's number was listed under the word *Ugh*, which was more polite than she and Speck deserved after some of their previous transgressions.

No second-guessing, Robin. I hit the call button.

In seconds, Clarice's voice spoke on the other end of the phone. "Hello?"

"It's Robin Wildwood."

She let out a squeal that caused me to hold the phone away from my ear for a moment. "Robin! What a lovely surprise."

"Hello, Clarice," I said. "I take it Speck's with you too?"

"Did you want to do another interview?" she said hopefully.

"Maybe," I hedged, "but I'll need a favour."

"Anything you like!"

"I want you to find any contacts you might have who found incriminating information on my aunt Shannon."

"You... want us to find contacts on Shannon Wildwood?" Her jubilant tone gained the slightest hesitancy. "Are you quite sure?"

"Yes, and the reasons aren't anything I'm willing to talk about over the phone," I said firmly. "I assume you still have contacts at the *Blue Moon*?"

"Yes… yes." She sounded as if she might faint from sheer delight. "Speck and I will ask everyone we know."

"Please try to be discreet," I added. "And definitely don't tell anyone *I'm* the one who asked. If you keep this to yourself, I'll give you an interview."

"Of course!" she said. "You know, we've heard all sorts of intriguing stories out of Wildwood Heath in the past few weeks! There's all manner of rumours around your mother's strange withdrawal from public life."

"I'll tell you more in the interview *if* you keep your word." There was no point in giving away all my secrets too early—if at all—and over my dead body would I tell her about Mum.

"Well… all right," she said. "It'll be so good to talk to you again!"

"One more thing," I said. "Can you also ask your contacts if they know of a coven called the Burdock Coven? Do you know the name?"

"Burdock?" A pause. "No, but I'll be sure to ask!"

"Thanks." I ended the call and pocketed my phone before returning to the table. Tansy sat guarding my seat, but someone had claimed Rowan's while she was occupied with juggling customers.

"Done already?" Tansy said. "I bet they practically wet themselves when they realised it was you."

"Accurate." I picked up what was left of my cold coffee. "I need a nap. Or a bath."

Spying me, Rowan made a beeline for the table. "They said yes?"

"Yeah." I crumpled the coffee cup in my fist. "I had to give them an incentive, but I made it clear that I wouldn't do an interview unless they brought me something concrete. I also didn't tell them about Mum, but they heard some rumour anyway. I guess it's par for the course in their line of business."

"You promised an interview in return?" she said. "If they do come through for you and you have to keep your word, how much will you share?"

I shrugged. "I'll ask Chloe to help. She's better at that kind of thing than I am."

I didn't know how she'd take the news, but unlike my brother, she wouldn't lambast me for making the decision. As for Ramsey… I'd have to avoid him for a while.

Rowan nodded. "If they want a second interviewee, I'm game. I have years of experience at surviving my mother."

"I know." I hoped I wouldn't regret asking them to pry into Linnea's coven, too, but I hadn't been able to resist bringing up the name. There'd almost certainly been a cover-up somewhere, and who better to pry open that door than a pair of the most persistent journalists in the region?

Tansy jumped onto my shoulder. "We'd better hope they find something *before* your aunt realises what we did."

Yeah. I was just thinking the same thing.

I walked back to the office slowly, putting off the moment when I'd have to admit what I'd done. Chloe would be understanding, but Grandma was another story. Hopefully, she was still sulking in the afterworld to avoid answering my questions. Between the reporters and the Wardens, I had more than one option to get to the truth regardless of whether she chose to share it with me.

At the coven headquarters, I spied Aunt Shannon's magpie familiar perched on the roof, though she took flight when Tansy made a threatening motion in that direction. I assumed that meant she hadn't overheard me talking with the reporters. My secret was safe from Aunt Shannon... for now.

While Tansy sat on magpie watch outside, I went into the office and found Chloe staring at the phone with a furrow in her brow.

"I can't get through to Jemima," she said. "She must be out. Or in a Head Witch meeting."

"Probably the latter," I replied. "I have something to tell you."

As expected, Chloe reacted with surprise but not outright shock when I revealed my call to the reporters.

"I did wonder if the press might have access to information that we don't," she said. "I don't like the idea, and your mother wouldn't, either, but I know our options are limited. Some of the other Head Witches might hesitate to come to your defence without irrefutable proof of your aunt's treachery."

"That's if the journalists can find it," I added. "I know I'm treading on shaky ground, but Ramsey pretty much bit my head off for suggesting I should go and gather allies in person or even meet with the local Wardens' branch."

"I expect he's worried about Leona," she said. "I don't think it's a bad idea to call the other Head Witches, but it's hard to prove to them that blackmail was involved in the council's support of Shannon when none of the others will admit to anything."

"Exactly," I said. "I promised an interview in exchange for the reporters' help, which might have been a mistake, but I couldn't think of anything else that would convince them to do as I asked."

"You don't have to give away too much," Chloe said. "You never promised to share every detail of what's going on in the coven, did you?"

"Luckily, no." The key was giving them enough enticing details that I didn't have to admit that Mum was in a coma or that I was on the brink of losing my title. Or anything about the demons. Really, the list of things I *could* talk about was shorter than the alternative, but I trusted Chloe to help me come up with a plan.

My brother was wrong. Having the support of others wasn't anything to be ashamed of. I didn't have to do this alone.

When I escaped the office at the day's end, I found a message from Piper on my phone saying that I had to call her back "RIGHT NOW."

Oh boy, Rowan told her.

I hit the call button. "Everything okay?"

"Your cousin told me," Piper said without preamble. "What in the hell are you thinking?"

"That my brother grounded me here, and I don't have a lot of options." I spoke in a low voice. "She *told* you? Please tell me that magpie wasn't hanging around."

"Nobody was listening," she replied. "I did tell her you wouldn't like her spreading the word—but seriously, *Clarice and Speck?* That's who you want to work with?"

"Like I said. Lack of options." I glanced around the street out of habit, but the only other animal around was Tansy. "It might not work out. If they don't find anything, I won't have to keep up my end of the bargain."

"They will," she said. "Your aunt's as squeaky-clean as an old broomstick, but that doesn't mean you need to let her command all your attention when you have other priorities."

"I can't ignore her," I murmured. "She blackmailed the council into helping her unseat me, and when I postponed her challenge, she persuaded them to stop coming in to work altogether."

Piper swore. "I know she's resorting to sketchy tactics. I just worry you'll land in even more trouble if you provoke her."

"So do I, believe me," I said. "I'd come and talk to you later, but I have a date with Harvey tonight."

"Right. Doesn't Harvey have to make up his mind on whether he's taking part in that regional championship thing soon?"

"Yeah." I'd almost forgotten. "Yeah… we need to talk about that."

I'd told him to say yes to the offer, but the recent developments might have given him second thoughts. As conflicted as my own feelings might be, I'd make it clear that none of my family drama would get in the way of his dreams.

An hour later, I met Harvey at our usual place in front of the Fox's Den. I'd texted him that I had news and he'd replied that he did, too, and we walked to our table with less cheer than usual. Tansy sat at our feet with her eyes on the door to make sure no magpies followed us in.

"You think your aunt is watching you?" he guessed.

"Almost certainly," I replied. "I doubt she's listening in for news on your career, though. Please tell me you said yes."

He nodded. "I asked the team, and the others unanimously voted to accept the invitation to take part in the championships. We agreed to go ahead with it."

"Oh, good," I said, though my heart twisted inside my chest. "You haven't actually accepted yet?"

"We have to give our answer tomorrow," he replied. "But… if we accept, the first preliminary match is next week."

My chest knotted even further. "I guess it makes sense to have the matches done before the end of summer."

"Sorry, Robin," he said. "I know the timing's not ideal. If you want me to turn them down…"

"No way," I said. "This is your dream. You've been waiting to take part in the championships for years." *Besides,* I added silently, *the demons aren't going to put their plans on hold if my boyfriend stays in town.*

"I wish you could come too," he admitted. "I know it's probably too risky for you to be at a public sports match outside of Wildwood Heath."

"You might say that." A sigh lodged in my throat. "My

brother has effectively grounded me now that the Wardens are actively hunting the demon."

His brows shot up. "He thinks Leona will come back?"

"If she notices she's being hunted," I said. "He may be right, but he's making it impossible for me to gather allies from outside of Wildwood Heath too. So I may have done something rash and called the reporters."

I relayed the details over dinner. The pub's food was delicious, but neither of us did much more than pick at our meals, too distracted by the implications of what we'd both revealed to focus on anything else.

"Are you sure you want to poke the bear?" Harvey asked when I'd finished recounting my call with Clarice and Speck.

"Clarice isn't a bear. More like a mouse."

"Definitely not a squirrel," Tansy put in. "I think he meant your aunt Shannon, though."

"She's more like a rabid manticore, but I can handle her."

"I'm sure you can." A worried frown creased his forehead. "Do you think any scandal is enough to bring her down? If she's blackmailing the council, they might feel obliged to keep up their support even if she turns out to have done something really heinous."

"They might have second thoughts if I put out the truth in an interview and call in the other Head Witches to back me up," I said. "Chloe's trying to get hold of them."

"She's a good assistant."

"She is," I agreed. "She didn't even panic too much when I told her I called the press."

"And your brother?" he said. "He doesn't know yet?"

I groaned. "No. He explicitly ordered me not to call the reporters, and I've gone back on my word, but being confined to town wasn't part of our agreement either. It's a mess, frankly."

"I bet." When I rested my head in my hands, he nudged

my elbow gently. "For the record, I don't think you made a rash decision."

"It's not the first I've made today. I may have stopped at my aunt's house to confront her too."

He winced. "How did that go?"

"Terribly." I lowered my hands. "I convinced Belinda to come back, but the others are entirely in her pocket, and at this rate, we'll get nothing done before my time runs out in a month and I have to face my aunt's challenge again."

"Will you tell the council you met with the press? If they unearth anything on your aunt, I mean?"

"I don't know." That was the honest answer.

"Not to put you under pressure," he added, "but the challenge your aunt brought to your title was due to you acting without the council's knowledge. If she gets wind of this…"

"The council stayed at home," I pointed out. "They can hardly blame me for anything they might have missed out on while they weren't around."

He was right, though. I was treading a fine line, and it'd take only one careless word to bring everything crashing down on my head. Aunt Shannon would inevitably find out. It was just a matter of when and where.

"I wasn't trying to undermine you," he said. "I just worry."

"You aren't the only one," I said. "My brother acted like the Wardens would turn around and stab us in the back even though he's the one who called them in the first place."

"The Reaper incident shook him up, right?"

"Don't remind me," I said. "That's what kicked this off. Tam called my brother to tell him that Linnea's mother used to be a coven leader, but the local Wardens wouldn't give any more details about her, and I can't ask them in person because my brother has decided it's too risky."

"A coven leader?" he asked. "Which coven?"

"The Burdocks." I spoke in a low voice. "Never heard of them, but they supposedly died out twenty years ago."

"You asked the reporters to look into that too?" he guessed.

"You've got it," I said. "I know Linnea isn't the priority, and there's a limit to what we can find out about the Reapers from the outside, but she wasn't always a Reaper. And her coven died out twenty years ago. Know what else happened around the same time?"

Comprehension widened his eyes. "The demons."

"Exactly," I said. "I've asked the reporters to focus on my aunt, first and foremost, but I'll consider it a bonus if they manage to find anything else."

There were plenty of stories on Aunt Shannon already out there. Compared to the Burdock Coven, she was a known quantity, and the tabloids had got years of material out of the mysterious death of her ex-husband alone. That'd been long enough ago that I didn't recall all the details, but if even suspected murder hadn't been able to destroy her reputation, what would?

Whatever works. Piper might not approve—and hell, *I* didn't approve—but to win this, I had to play her game for a bit.

And hope I didn't lose my soul in the process.

———

I spent the night at Harvey's. Not usually a good idea on a weeknight, but I needed the company, and if I admitted it, I was also doing my level best to avoid facing Ramsey. I was pretty sure he'd spent the night at the police station regardless, and there were worse ways to wake up than to Harvey bringing me coffee in bed.

"Thanks." I blew on my coffee to cool it down. "You're the best."

My phone started to buzz, and the word *Ugh* flashed across the screen. With instincts honed from years of Sky Hopper practise, Harvey lunged and grabbed my coffee before I dropped it in my mad scramble to pick up the phone. "Yes?"

"Robin!" Clarice's squeal was entirely too loud for this hour in the morning. "Sorry it's so early, but I just couldn't wait to speak to you!"

"I assume you have good reason?" I glanced out of the window instinctively, though Tansy had taken her guard duty seriously and had been vigilantly watching the skies for anything magpie-shaped. Not that I thought my aunt would go as far as to creep on Harvey and me sleeping, but one never knew.

"Yes," Clarice said breathlessly. "We managed to get in touch with a journalist who once worked at the *Blue Moon* and who wrote a story concerning your aunt. A story so scandalous it was never printed!"

"What story?"

"We don't know," she said. "Unfortunately, he refused to give us the details, but we think he'll speak to *you*, Head Witch. If you speak to him in person."

"No." I couldn't leave town. Not just because of my brother's warning but because going to meet a stranger alone was the height of foolishness even if I was armed with my sceptre. "Can I call him instead?"

"He doesn't have a phone," she said. "He said there's too big a risk of someone putting a spell on the line and eavesdropping. He won't risk your aunt finding out where he lives. He seems terrified of her."

Oh boy. "Are you sure he'll even talk to me?"

"Quite sure." She dropped her voice. "I believe your aunt

may have persuaded him not to share the story, but if you explain that you're intending to challenge her…"

Right. "I'll think about it."

"And the interview?"

Of course that was what she was building up to. "Wait until I've spoken to him. *If* I speak to him."

"You won't regret it," she promised. "His name is Lloyd Burton. I'll send his address."

"Thanks." Terrified of my aunt, was he? That sounded like he'd got up close and personal with her blackmail methods, but was it worth risking worse to speak to the guy face-to-face?

I ended the call. Harvey handed me back my coffee. "Clarice, was it?"

"She found someone with a story on my aunt that was too outrageous to make it into print," I explained. "Unfortunately, he's unwilling to talk to anyone except me, and he wants to speak in person."

"He won't come here?"

"Definitely not, since my aunt seems to have threatened him so badly that he won't even use a phone." I sighed. "I know it's a terrible idea on all levels, but what story was too bad for the *Blue Moon* to publish? They accused her of murdering her husband several times."

"Good question." His brow creased. "If you want me to come with you, I'd be happy to be your backup."

"Would you?" Did I want to risk putting him in danger too? "I'll ask Chloe's advice first. She knows about the plan already."

She also needed to know I was going to give the *Blue Moon* an interview if this guy turned out to be genuine, which meant we needed a strategy ASAP.

After a hasty breakfast, I walked from Harvey's house to the coven headquarters. Tansy scampered at my side, offering up absurd theories on what Aunt Shannon had done.

"No, she didn't start a cult, Tansy," I said to my familiar. "I mean… she *might* have, but it's not that big a deal compared to some of the alternatives."

"It is if she performed human sacrifice."

"I don't think that's likely, Tansy."

Upon reaching the coven headquarters, I entered the office and found Chloe already sitting at her desk.

"You know you don't have to show up this early," I told her. "There's not that much to do."

"There is," she insisted. "I can't reach any of the Head Witches on the phone."

"What?" My heart missed a beat. "Not just Jemima?"

"Nor Mavis either," she said. "I think there's another spell on the phone lines, preventing anyone in the office from contacting the other Head Witches."

"Aunt Shannon." I swore. "Can't you call them from somewhere else?"

"The number won't even work on my personal phone," she said. "I don't know what she did, but it's powerful magic."

A chill raced down my arms. "Speaking of her crimes, Clarice and Speck put me in touch with someone who wrote a story on my aunt a few years ago that was so scandalous that it made him morbidly terrified of her. He wants to meet me in person and won't risk speaking to anyone else."

"What?" Her eyes rounded. "You can't leave town."

"Didn't you just say we can't reach the Head Witches?" I set the sceptre beside my desk in its usual spot. "She's not going to stop there, you know that. I have to expose her. Besides, Harvey offered to come with me."

Her expression clouded. "I don't know… didn't you also promise an interview in exchange?"

"I did," I admitted. "But only after I get the story. Not before."

"All right." She opened her laptop. "If you like, I can write you a script for the interview. To make sure you don't give away anything you don't want to."

"Seriously?"

Chloe nodded. "I can write some prompt cards too. Whatever works best."

"Good idea." Chloe had my back, and her support was as valuable as her skills as an assistant. "That'll be a real help."

"It's no problem," she said. "I'll write the script and then see if I can disentangle whatever spell your aunt cast on the phone lines."

"It's got to be a sophisticated one if she tangled up *your* phone too."

"I don't think she did," said Chloe. "I think the spell is on either the building itself or part of town. It's not tied to one individual phone."

"I hope it isn't." She sure hadn't touched *my* phone. My heart began racing all the same when I pulled it out and saw my call history. Maybe I ought to have borrowed someone else's phone to call the press. If she'd seen…

"It's not on yours. Don't worry." She caught sight of my face. "I can try Jemima's number if you like."

"Sure." I held out my phone so she could type in her number, but after a moment, she shook her head.

"I think she used some kind of security ward," Chloe said. "Like an invisible shield."

"That specifically keeps us from reaching the Head Witches?" Damn, she was smart. "Would you be able to make the call from the other side of town?"

Wildwood Heath didn't have the best phone reception anyway, but my aunt had apparently been researching tech spells as in-depth as she had the coven's rule book. This certainly wasn't anything I'd learned at school, including the classes I'd slept through.

"I might," she said doubtfully. "I'll go back to the interview script, and we'll try that later."

Our back-and-forth over the interview script took the whole morning. I'd expected at least one interruption from Grandma, but none came, which was kind of a relief given our plan.

"I think we're going to have to tell them Mum was injured," I said. "That's the only way to explain the loophole Aunt Shannon used to snag her coven leader title."

"All right, but we won't let on that she's in a coma," said Chloe. "That's too much."

"Yeah." My heart gave a twinge. Would Mum see this as a betrayal when she eventually woke up?

I don't have a choice. The script would help, but in truth, I didn't know whether I'd be able to restrain myself from being honest when I was in the hot seat.

At lunchtime, I messaged both Rowan and Piper and asked them to meet me at the café. The former would already be there, of course, but I didn't want to explain the plan several times and risk being overheard. Tansy had had to chase Myrtle away from my office window seven times so far, as she told me when I met her at the door.

"I'm sure Piper and Rowan won't like my plan, but I figured I should let them in on it anyway," I said to her.

"You haven't actually called Clarice and Speck back to confirm you're going ahead to see this journalist guy, have you?" Tansy asked.

"No." I needed to do that, too, but first, I wanted to ensure there was a plan in place to keep my aunt from discovering where I'd gone.

Rowan wasn't working today, and it was a simple matter to corner her and whisper my dilemma into her ear.

She blanched. "You can't go there in person. No way."

"I have to," I said. "He'll only speak to me, and he's too scared to use a phone because of your mother."

Which, given my aunt's recent manoeuvre with the coven's phone lines, might not have been all that irrational.

Rowan grimaced. "I… I have no idea what story he's got on my mother. Twenty years ago, you say? Isn't that around the time when…?"

"When the demons attacked," I said. "And when Linnea's mother died too."

"I don't like coincidences. What if someone's setting you up?"

"Harvey offered to come with me," I said. "This guy seems a little paranoid, but we both know Clarice and Speck. They're morally slippery, but not compared to…"

"My mother, I know." She glanced around the café, her gaze lingering on the tables. "She'll know if you leave."

"Harvey and I will think of an alibi," I said. "We can pretend we're visiting locations for his upcoming tour with the Sky Hopper team."

"Robin." Ramsey's sharp voice cut through Rowan's reply. My brother stood in the doorway, his expression incandescent.

This is not going to be pretty.

8

"**H**ey." I tried to sound casual. I really did.

"Robin." Ramsey exhaled in a sigh. "I'd like you to come outside and talk to me."

"I'm talking to Rowan." I also had the sense that if I stayed put, his head might actually explode in rage. *He knows what I did... but how? Who gave the game away?*

"Now." He put on his most serious police officer voice, the sort that reached the far corners of an empty room and caused everyone to turn in his direction. I got the message and followed him outside.

When he veered towards the police station, I slowed. "Am I being arrested?"

"No, but a stint in a cell might stop you from endangering your life." He spoke through gritted teeth. "I can't believe you'd consider working with the same reporters who shamed and harassed our family—to say nothing of unknown journalists with an agenda of their own."

"Let me guess… your familiar was spying on me?"

"No, of course not."

"Then who?" Wait. "Not Chloe."

"No… Grandma."

My mouth fell open. "She left the office?"

"She did," he confirmed. "She came into the house just before I left for work and told me that you intended to betray us."

"She never told *me* that." That's what I got for assuming she was too busy sulking to eavesdrop on Chloe and me while we made our plans. "If she'd been honest with me, I might not have had to go behind her back to learn the truth."

"This isn't about our grandmother," he said. "This is your attempt to win against our aunt, at the cost of your own safety and that of everyone around you."

"I'm going to meet a journalist, not confront the demon," I pointed out. "The Wardens haven't actually found Leona yet, have they?"

"Yes," he said. "They have."

Well. *Now* he told me. "When did you find that out?"

"They left me a voicemail message late last night." He studied me through narrowed eyes. "I'm not going to pretend I understand why you're willing to risk both your safety and your family's for the sake of scoring points against our aunt, but I'm frankly shocked that Chloe went along with it."

All right, that was unfair. "It's not about scoring points. It's about stopping her from stealing the sceptre. Does it not matter to you that she already stole Mum's title?"

"That doesn't justify endangering yourself," he said. "To say nothing of the message it'll send to other unscrupulous individuals who want to exploit our family's secrets."

"It's one interview, in exchange for a favour," I said, irked. "We made a deal. Like you did with the Wardens."

"Robin, this is out of the question."

"Aren't you a little bit curious what Aunt Shannon did that was too outrageous to put in print?" I asked. "What's worse than all the stories of her murdering her husband?"

"If I were you, Robin, I wouldn't ask that question."

Does he already know? Was he somehow in on the secret? Surely not. "I'm not playing games, Ramsey. There's a very real chance Aunt Shannon will get our entire family killed in her bid for power. I'm happy to put myself on the line if it means stopping her."

"And Harvey too?"

He had to go there. I folded my arms across my chest. "What, would you prefer that I go to meet this guy alone?"

"No, that you go with me."

I stared at him, fighting a laugh. "You know, jokes usually have a punch line."

"I'm serious, Robin," he said. "If you're not going to give ground, I'd prefer that you go to meet this man in the company of someone trustworthy."

"Did you just imply Harvey isn't trustworthy?" I asked before I could help myself.

"No." He pinched the bridge of his nose between his fingertips. "He's not trained to fight demons."

Neither are you. Though if it meant he refrained from locking me in a cell to keep me from leaving town, I'd happily play along. "You really think that the town needs to be without its Head Witch *and* the head of the police at the same time?"

"The police will be fine," he said. "As for you, the coven won't notice you're gone, not if you cover your tracks."

"Cover my tracks?" I echoed. "You know, Aunt Shannon already figured out we met with the Wardens. Tansy spent half the past few days chasing that magpie away, and it still wasn't enough."

"Tansy is going to help." He turned to my familiar. "Sorry, but you'll have to stay behind if you want Robin's alibi to be convincing."

"I'll do no such thing!" Tansy said haughtily. "You can't leave me at home."

My heart sank. "Tansy… that probably is how she knew I was gone before. You're very conspicuous—don't look at me like that. It's not an insult. I just mean you draw so much attention that it's easy to tell when you're not around."

She flopped onto her back. "You're breaking my heart."

"You're proving my point." I crouched beside her. "I hate the idea of leaving you behind. You know that. But if there's no other way to fool Aunt Shannon…"

"You can come up with an alibi for Robin." Ramsey crouched beside me. "You can lead Aunt Shannon on a wild goose chase."

"Or squirrel chase," I added, inspired. "I can guarantee it'll be worth staying behind to have the chance to wind her up."

She flipped the right way up. "I guess."

"It'll be fun." I let her jump onto my shoulder and rose upright when I spied Piper running down the street.

"Hey, Robin," she said. "Sorry I got tied up… what's going on?"

I looked between her and my familiar. "I might need your help too."

———

The meeting was set for the following morning. Clarice and Speck had been delighted when I'd called them back to confirm that I was going ahead with the plan and that I'd give them an interview if what the journalist told me was satisfactory.

It had better be, given all the time it took my friends and I to plan a diversion, supervised by my ever-picky brother. We'd thrown out a dozen plans before we'd settled on me using the sceptre to create an illusory copy of myself walking to work with Tansy that Piper would supervise in case it randomly disappeared or something. Illusion magic was tricky, but the sceptre's power ought to be able to pull it off, and Rowan and Piper would be on standby if anything went awry.

The two weren't exactly the best of friends, but shared a mutual interest in helping to protect me. Harvey too. When I'd dropped the news that I'd be going to meet the reporter with my brother instead, I'd done so with a mixture of guilt at leaving him behind and relief that he wouldn't be exposed to the same potential dangers.

Ramsey, though… I didn't have the faintest idea what had been going through his head when he'd agreed to come with me. Part of me expected him to change his mind by morning, but he didn't, and he woke me up before my alarm by rapping on my door loudly enough that I groaned. "Not necessary, Ramsey."

"We'll have to leave as early as possible if you want your substitute to go into work without drawing suspicion" was his reply.

"At least he's still on board with the plan," Tansy remarked from her perch on the bed frame. "I wondered if *he'd* been replaced by a clone when he agreed to this."

"Speaking of clones, I hope my sceptre can create a copy of me that's good enough to fool Aunt Shannon."

After I dressed and went downstairs to grab a quick breakfast, Piper showed up, dressed in her muddiest clothes under the pretext of having come to work in Mum's garden. "Ready?"

"Nope." I shoved a last piece of toast into my mouth and picked up the sceptre, walking into the living room so I'd have more space. "Heard from Rowan?"

"She's got her familiar hiding in a gutter, watching for magpies."

"Good call." I checked my phone and sent Harvey a message telling him I was good to go. Then I lifted the sceptre in both hands. "I've never created a double of myself before. Knowing the sceptre, I won't be able to get rid of it afterwards. What then?"

"You can sleep in while your clone goes to work," Tansy said.

"You know, that's not the worst outcome." I glanced out of the window out of habit, but I'd heard noises an hour or so earlier that suggested Tansy and Horace had tag-teamed to chase Myrtle off. "Not sure my clone will be any better at paperwork than I am, but it's worth a shot."

Go time. I waved the sceptre in a complex figure-eight motion and then up and down, following Piper's miming. She'd memorised the spell the previous day, on my brother's instruction, so there'd be minimal chance of any screw-ups.

Up, down... go.

Sparks flew then smoke, which billowed out in front of me and covered an area about as tall as I was. The smoke turned semitransparent, as if I was looking through a tinted window, and then shimmered like a mirror.

Inside the mirror, a copy of myself stood holding an identical copy of the sceptre. The other Robin's eyes looked into mine, and a chill raced through my veins. *Oh, wow.*

As I lowered the sceptre, the mirror-like surface melted away, leaving the copy of myself standing in the middle of the living room. "Whoa."

"Whoa," repeated the illusion.

"That's… different."

The clone repeated my words. I looked to my brother. "How do I stop her doing that?"

While she echoed me again, he shook his head. "I've never seen a spell like that used with a sceptre either."

"Now he tells me." Not that it was a surprise. Grandma

wouldn't have had any reason to create a copy of herself. She wouldn't have wanted the competition.

"Now he tells me," said the clone.

I swivelled to Ramsey. "You don't think she'll repeat everything I say when we're not actually in close proximity to each other, do you?"

"I'll cast a silencing spell if she does," Piper offered.

"Might be an improvement," said Tansy.

"Oi."

My familiar flicked me with her tail. "Your mother is going to kill both of you."

"No need to sound so cheerful." I rolled my eyes and ignored the clone's echo of my words. "Right… no time like the present. Are you sure you'll be okay staying behind?"

"No, I'm mortally insulted, but I'll survive." Tansy positioned herself next to my clone's feet. "Ready to go?"

"Yeah." I turned to Ramsey. "You definitely know the way?"

I'd passed on the journalist's address, and Ramsey had used his impeccable research skills to find out how to get there, but since Lloyd Burton had flat out refused to send a picture of his house, using a transportation spell risked us ending up somewhere else altogether. Those spells were more precise when you travelled to a place you'd already visited, but flying would be out of the question if we wanted our alibi to be believable.

Ramsey lifted his wand. "Let's go."

To travel in tandem and actually arrive in the same place, it was easier if we were touching one another, so I reached for his free hand and lifted the sceptre with the other.

The living room disappeared, and so did my clone. In its place, we stood on a country lane that led down into a village that might have been a carbon copy of any other paranormal community I'd visited. Ramsey began to walk downhill towards the cluster of houses as if he'd been here a dozen times.

"How do you know where we're going?" I wished the sceptre wasn't so conspicuous. The glowing purple light stood out like a beacon amid the deserted fields. "It looks like every other paranormal village in the region."

"This isn't a paranormal community," he corrected. "It shows up on regular maps. That's how I found it."

"You did?" I raised a brow. "Don't tell the journalist that. I got the impression that he's trying to be anonymous." Namely, to avoid Aunt Shannon.

Hoping my clone was behaving itself back at home, I followed my brother downhill until we reached the village.

Lloyd Burton lived in a modest-sized detached house set apart from its neighbours by hedges thick enough that I couldn't see much of the actual property. A tall gate at the front blocked our way, and I halted outside, uncertain. "How're we meant to let him know we're here?"

The hedges moved, leaves rustling, and then the gates began to creak inward as though pulled by an invisible pair of hands. When a gap large enough to step through was revealed, a voice whispered, "Come in, Head Witch."

"That's not ominous at all." I wished Tansy was with me. Her fluffy tail wrapped around my shoulders would be a real comfort right now. "Are you Lloyd Burton?"

No answer came, but something sharp and sudden prodded me in the spine, causing me to trip over the threshold. Ramsey moved forward, too, but the gates were already closing behind me, leaving my brother stranded on the other side.

I looked to see what had poked me and saw that the hedges had sprouted what appeared to be a pair of arms that ended in spines instead of hands.

"Who is that?" asked an equally bristly voice that sounded

like it was coming through a speaker. "I was told the Head Witch was coming alone."

"My brother's here for moral support," I said to the voice, assuming its owner was inside the house. "You'd better not hurt him."

Or me. I gripped the sceptre with both hands as I walked down the short path to the front door, which swung open like the gate had. Inside the living room on the other side was a surprisingly short man with thinning hair, half crouched beside some contraption that looked like a giant cannon painted bright purple.

It was also pointed directly at me.

"What...?" I tensed as the door snapped closed, trapping me in the same room as the cannon's owner. Who, I realised too late, might not be entirely sane.

"Put down your weapon," said Lloyd Burton. "My security spells will keep pointing at you until you do."

"All right, all right." I didn't *want* to put down the sceptre, but death by magical cannon was not my idea of a good time either. Sidestepping, I rested the sceptre against the wall where I could see it and released a breath when the cannon turned away.

Lloyd Burton extended a hand. "It's nice to meet you, Robin."

"I might have said the feeling was mutual, but..." I gestured to the cannon and then realised I'd blown all chances of making a good first impression. Really, though, who wouldn't be at least mildly freaked out about this situation? "Are you usually this paranoid?"

"Yes," he said without any hint of shame. "Your brother is the head of the law enforcement in Wildwood Heath, isn't he?"

"I couldn't come here alone," I said. "My life is in danger."

"So is mine," he said.

"I doubt we're facing the same threat." I fixed him with a stare. "I risked my life in coming here because I was told you had a story about Shannon Wildwood that never appeared in print. I want to know what it is, and I want it shared publicly."

"No." He blanched. "I said I'd tell you my story, yes, but I can't share it publicly. I can't."

We'll see. "Hypothetically, would you change your mind if you knew that Shannon Wildwood had taken power over the entire Wildwood Coven and was also on her way to stealing the title of Head Witch? What if you were the one person who can prevent her from doing that?"

His knees buckled, and he sat down on the sofa. "You can't be serious."

"I am." I spoke clearly. "I won't let your name be associated with the story if you don't want me to, but I need to know what she did. Given that the *Blue Moon* once printed a series of stories speculating on her murdering her ex-husband, I find it hard to believe you found anything worse."

"I…" he trailed off. "This was a bad idea. I shouldn't have invited you to come, but Clarice and Speck said you weren't like the other Head Witch."

He means Grandma. "What's that supposed to mean? I've already told you more than I should have."

It wasn't hard to imagine my brother glaring at me through the curtained window, telling me not to be so open with him, but I silently replied, *Does he look like a threat to you?*

"I… fine." He took in a breath, his gaze fixed on the floor. "Twenty years ago, Shannon Wildwood's husband was involved in an extramarital affair with a prominent figure in another coven. I was new to journalism at the time and was sent to report on the story for the *Blue Moon*. I didn't expect…"

"Didn't expect what?" Aunt Shannon's husband had

cheated. Everyone knew that. But admittedly I hadn't known the person he'd absconded with had belonged to a coven outside of the Wildwoods. Not that anyone at home had dared ask too many questions at the time, or so I thought.

He gave a shudder. "I went to their headquarters to spy, and I found them dabbling in… in… terrible illegal magic."

"Illegal, like…?" I didn't say the word "necromancy," but that was the first thing to come to mind. There was a lot more to illegal magic than that, of course, but a sense of foreboding gripped me. "Did they summon anything?"

"How did you know?" His head snapped upward, panic flaring in his eyes.

"Guesswork. Go on." I watched him until his gaze lowered.

He continued in a whisper. "I didn't realise what they were doing at first. He was with them too. Her… her husband. He'd been invited in."

"Not Aunt Shannon, though," I guessed. "If she wasn't involved in the illegal magic herself, why would she have a problem with you printing the story?"

"Because of what happened afterwards." He took in a shaky breath. "I went back to the *Blue Moon*'s office, and they told me to try to get closer and bring actual video footage as proof. But the next time I visited… that was when Shannon Wildwood found out and came to confront her husband face-to-face."

Oh boy. "Did she know they were dabbling in illegal magic too?"

"Not at first." He spoke quietly. "The coven… they had something captured in the downstairs room. When I looked through the window, I saw… monsters."

My heart swooped downward. "What, demons?"

"I don't know," he said. "I wanted to flee, but I did as my employer asked and stayed to see what I could catch on camera. It was because I was that close that I heard the fight break out between Shannon Wildwood and her husband."

My skin crawled. "Then what?"

He squeezed his eyes shut. "The fight was terrible. The whole house was shaking, and the quake... it brought down whatever was keeping those creatures contained."

Oh. Oh *no.* "They escaped?"

"Yes." He swallowed hard. "They did, and she... and Shannon Wildwood fled the house. I saw her. She used magic to lock the door behind her."

My heart gave an uneasy jolt. "She locked her husband in a house with a demon?"

"Her husband, the coven leader... everyone." He faltered. "I fled as fast as I could, but your aunt ran in the same direction, and she saw my camera. She might have killed me on the spot if we hadn't encountered the Head Witch coming the other way."

"Grandma."

It couldn't have been anyone else. She'd known all along what her younger daughter had done, but would she have told me without prompting? Doubtful. I'd always known Aunt Shannon was far from the pinnacle of moral fortitude, but locking people inside a house with a rampaging demonic horde was a step over the line even for her.

"What was the coven's name?" I asked, though I already knew the answer. "Was the coven leader... was she the person who was involved with my aunt's husband?"

"Yes." His lips moved, the word barely audible. "The name... was the Burdock Coven. None survived."

A chill broke out on my arms. "My grandmother knew. The last Head Witch, I mean."

"I assumed the previous Head Witch didn't want the story to spread. I never asked."

"No. She definitely didn't." That she'd managed to stifle

the news of an entire coven going up in smoke was an impressive feat, though plainly, the Wardens had found out anyway. Maybe someone had called them to tidy up the aftermath. Grandma might not have banished all the monsters herself, but she'd done enough to earn a lifetime grudge.

"What happened when you took the story back to the *Blue Moon?*" I asked.

He shuddered again. "I got back and found the whole office was on fire. All our equipment was ruined. The others thought it was an accident, but I knew better."

My heart lurched. "What then?"

"I went home, and… found the place burned to the ground."

Damn. Now I was starting to see why he'd moved here to the middle of nowhere. "That's when you went into hiding?"

"I've been here ever since."

The implication was clear. If I shared the story publicly, he expected to lose his home… or worse. What was I supposed to do? Aunt Shannon… I could hardly believe she'd *been* there, she'd witnessed the demons' escape, and she'd done nothing to help the innocent people of the surrounding village, who surely hadn't known of their leading coven's dangerous hobby.

Yes, the demons might have already killed them all before my grandmother had shown up to help, but Linnea… even if she didn't directly know how her mother had died, she certainly knew where to place the blame. That must have been why Aunt Shannon had prepared in advance of Linnea's betrayal, why she'd met with the council and planted the seeds of her plan to unseat me. She hadn't known Mum would end up in a coma, surely, but she hadn't needed a crystal ball to figure out that Linnea would target both Mum and me.

Nice of her to warn me. I took in a breath. "Thanks for telling me. I know it must have been hard."

He flinched a little. "You won't share the story with anyone else, will you?"

I can't let this poor guy keep living in fear forever. "You did hear me say that Shannon Wildwood is a danger to everyone, didn't you? She's blackmailed her way into power, and the only thing that might unseat her is a story that even she can't talk her way out of."

"You don't know that."

"I know her, Lloyd," I said. "I'm related to her, remember?"

Also, he'd seemingly forgotten that he had the head of Wildwood Heath's police department stuck outside his house. Someone who would *not* walk away from here without getting the story for himself.

"You said she's a danger to everyone," he said. "She's not someone you want in power, no, but—it's not her you're afraid of, is it? You implied…"

"Demons." Might as well lay out all my cards while I was at it. "The demons that escaped and killed the Burdock Coven are back for revenge on my grandmother, and since she's dead, the sceptre chose me to finish what she started. Aunt Shannon wants the sceptre, too, not to fight the demons but for her own ambitions. My mother was put into a coma fighting against the surviving daughter of one of those coven members who died when that demon attacked. You can probably guess what happened next."

He gaped at me. "The… the Wildwood Coven's leader is in a coma?"

Oops. I probably shouldn't have given quite *that* much away. "Now do you understand? If I don't put out that story, I won't be able to stop my aunt from stealing the sceptre. I don't know about you, but I wouldn't want her to be the last line of defence between the coven and a bunch of demons."

He made a choked noise. "That's unfair."

"So is the fact that you've been forced to live in isolation for decades," I pointed out. "I can help you, but only if you let me share your story. The only name on it will be mine."

He fidgeted. "I don't want any of this traced back to me."

"It won't be, unless…" I thought. "Do you still have the footage?"

"I had the camera with me when my office burned down," he mumbled. "It's hidden away in a safe."

"That's proof," I said. "More proof than just words. Can I see it?"

He shook his head. "If she—if Shannon sees the footage, she'll know I'm the one who filmed it. I'm the only journalist who was at the scene."

Tricky. "Nobody knows you still have the camera, do they? I can claim it was in the Wardens' secure safe or something and that they picked it up after you dropped it while running for your life."

When he shook his head again, I said, "Look, we can do this all morning, but my brother's outside, and he's probably plotting a rescue mission to get me out. Fair warning."

"I can't bring the police into this."

"Ramsey knows how to keep a secret," I said. "Tell you what, you can talk to him yourself. Don't worry. His bark is worse than his bite."

9

After another showdown with the magical cannon, Ramsey and the journalist talked for nearly an hour. I left them to it and went to get some air, wishing I had my familiar with me. She'd be hopping mad to have missed out on this, though she wouldn't have appreciated the spiky hedges. No wonder there weren't any animals in the garden. The place was utterly quiet.

In the absence of any other ideas as to how to occupy myself, I called Clarice and Speck. I figured I might as well work out the details of our interview while I was away from Wildwood Heath and any potential eavesdroppers.

When I hit the dial button, the hedge brandished a clawed hand at me and knocked my phone out of my grip.

"Hey!" I bent to pick it up. "I'm calling Clarice and Speck. They're friends with Lloyd."

I didn't know if it understood me, but when I lifted my phone to my ear, its arm-like branches retracted.

"Hello?" said Clarice's voice on the other end. "Is that you, Robin?"

"I was talking to the hedge," I said hastily, not sure if she'd heard the end of our altercation. "Did you know this guy's place is locked up tighter than the paranormal hunters' prison cells?"

"You already spoke to him?" Clarice exclaimed. "We'd be happy to do the interview at any time. Are you free today?"

Straight to the point, then. "I might be," I hedged. "My brother's still talking to Lloyd. I'm not sure he'll want us doing the interview from here, but I can't let you come to Wildwood Heath."

"Oh, we're happy to talk to you anywhere!" she said. "You pick the location."

"Anywhere, you say?" If my brother did somehow convince Lloyd to hand over the video footage, I'd be better off showing it to them in person, and I wouldn't get many other chances to leave Wildwood Heath anytime soon. "How about Yarrowfield?" I named the paranormal town I'd lived in during my last stint of normal-person employment, before Grandma's death had dragged me back to Wildwood Heath. I did still technically have access to my apartment there, though I'd had to have some slightly awkward calls with my landlord and boss after I'd gained the position of Head Witch.

"We know how to get there!" she said. "Let us know what time."

"I'll see if Ramsey's finished with Lloyd yet." Given that I hadn't heard any cannons go off, he couldn't have freaked out the journalist too badly, but it was difficult to tell from outside.

I ended the call and returned to the house. The door opened without me having to knock, revealing Lloyd holding an old-fashioned camera and Ramsey facing him with an outstretched hand.

"If you let me borrow that camera, it'll be all the proof I

need," Ramsey said to him. "I won't allow the footage to be widely spread."

"It should be," I interjected. "If we don't share it publicly, how is anyone supposed to trust that we're telling the truth? The *Blue Moon* isn't exactly a respected publication."

"And if Shannon knows we have the footage?" Ramsey countered. "That's enough on its own."

"Blackmail." I raised a brow at my brother. "Didn't know you had it in you, Ramsey."

Ramsey scowled. "I didn't say anything about black-mailing her. Did I hear you making a phone call outside?"

"Yes. I called Clarice and Speck," I said. "Can I show *them* the footage?"

Lloyd gave me a suspicious look. "Why?"

"Because they're going to write up your story as part of our interview." With luck, the journalist's story would take some of their attention off me and stop them from prying too deeply into my coven's current drama. "You trust them, don't you? You must if they know your address."

"We worked together, but that's not the same as letting them share... *that.*"

"Like I said, my name will be attached, not yours." I didn't need the video footage for the interview, but I wouldn't have put it past my aunt to try some trickery to stop the story getting out there. The more proof we had, the better.

"I... fine." He flinched when my brother took the camera from his hands, but he didn't move to take it back. "You'll bring it back to me when you're done?"

"Yes, if you give me a way to contact you that doesn't involve showing up on the doorstep or communicating via Clarice and Speck."

"Shannon Wildwood is dangerous," he mumbled. "You must know it."

"Oh, I do," I said. "Believe me."

Without further ado, Ramsey and I left the house with the camera and crossed the garden to the front gate. The hedge's arm-like protrusions reappeared to prod us over the threshold, just in case we didn't get the message.

"Ow." I rubbed my back with a hand as the gates closed behind us. "I wonder why he trusts Clarice and Speck more than us."

"You shouldn't have told him about Mum," Ramsey said.

"That's your first objection?" I asked. "You aren't a little more concerned by the fact that Aunt Shannon is at least partly responsible for pretty much all our current problems, including Linnea's grudge and the demons' fixation on our family?"

"She wasn't the one who summoned the demons."

"No, she wasn't," I allowed, "but I can see why Linnea pinned the blame on our coven for her mother's death. She'd have been a kid at the time, I bet."

Ramsey's mouth pressed into a thin line. "Regardless, it's risky telling a journalist anything that might offer ammunition to use against us."

"He won't share anything. He thinks Aunt Shannon will have him killed for it." I grimaced. "His life is pretty much in your hands now."

"No, it's in yours." He eyed the sceptre pointedly.

"Thanks for the reminder." He was right, though. No witness protection plan would get in my aunt's way if she wanted to finish him off permanently.

No pressure, then, Robin.

"What exactly did you tell Clarice and Speck on the phone?" he enquired. "Did you say you'd do the interview in person?"

"Today, yes," I replied. "Since we're already out of town. They let me pick the location, and I've chosen Yarrowfield, where I used to live."

"You *lived* there?"

"Technically, I still do." I sometimes forgot myself, admittedly, given that I'd been in Wildwood Heath full-time for months now. "I figured it's safe enough. People don't know I'm Head Witch there."

He still didn't look too pleased. "You don't have to do this in person."

"I have the footage." I indicated the camera in his hands. "Maybe if they see that, they'll be sufficiently freaked out not to do anything that'll draw Aunt Shannon's ire."

"We haven't even watched it ourselves."

"We have time." I lifted the sceptre. "Do you know how to get to Yarrowfield?"

"I'll come with you." We hadn't brought broomsticks, so transportation spells were our only way, and I kept my fingers mentally crossed that I didn't accidentally transport us into a tree.

In a flash, we vanished from outside Lloyd's house and landed in a street that looked both familiar and odd. My old apartment was on the first floor of a three-storey block that might have been mistaken for a regular non-paranormal building if not for the broomstick someone had left on the bike rack outside. Ramsey's gaze raked over the worn bricks and dirty windows. "This is it? It seems… small."

"I didn't spend a lot of time at home," I said defensively. "I was a courier, remember?"

"Right." From his tone, it was obvious that he'd forgotten I'd even *had* a job or a home in my previous life. Another reminder that family members didn't really think of my other life as a life at all. To them, nothing existed but Wildwood Heath.

"Nobody's here," I added. "The landlord hasn't rented out the place again because I paid to the end of my lease. You're welcome."

I'd only been able to afford *that* because of my new Head Witch salary, and I'd done my level best to keep the details from everyone I'd known here. Nobody in the building knew the Wildwood name.

I approached the front door and peered through the grimy glass, conscious of my brother's presence behind me.

"Yes, I figured you'd find plenty of things to criticise," I said over my shoulder, "but I'd appreciate it if you kept them to yourself."

Maybe I wasn't being fair. He *had* come with me, after all, and he'd even gone on this detour that hadn't been on the original plan.

"You always planned to come back here," he observed.

"That was implied." *Will I?* I hadn't intended to put down roots in Wildwood Heath again, but as I took in the narrow corridor lined with dull-brown doors on the other side of the door, I couldn't picture myself back in this world either. Too much had changed.

"But not anymore?" he guessed.

Instead of voicing my conflicting thoughts, I shrugged. "I might not survive long enough for it to matter."

A pause. "I thought you were staying in Wildwood Heath long enough to get rid of the sceptre and then leaving. Isn't that your priority?"

"If I just wanted to get rid of the sceptre, I'd have handed it to Aunt Shannon at the first opportunity, wouldn't I?" I didn't need to wait for an answer. "No, I'm going to fight the demon. I'm pretty sure we're all going to die in the process, but I'm not letting her be the one to dictate how it happens."

"We won't die," he said. "The Wardens will help."

"You said they'd found Leona?"

"Robin!" Clarice came running down the street in her bright-red cloak, Speck close behind her, laden with the usual array of recording equipment. "Is this the place?"

"There." I nodded to the building. "We'll go inside."

As I put in the entry code—that hadn't changed either—my brother whispered, "You really want them to have your address?"

"Like I said, I don't think it'll matter for long."

We climbed a staircase that smelled as if someone had used it as a toilet and reached the first floor. When I fished out my old spare key from under the doormat, Ramsey looked askance at me. "You left your key here?"

"What?" I whispered. "I didn't leave anything valuable behind."

The one-room studio flat had been half furnished when I'd moved in, and I'd bought the battered sofa and two armchairs secondhand. I didn't care what the two reporters thought of my old accommodation, and my brother would have found something to criticise even if I'd been living it up in a penthouse suite, so I sat in one of the armchairs to watch Clarice and Speck set up their equipment.

I wish Tansy was here.

"Robin," Ramsey whispered. "Didn't your assistant give you a script?"

"Oh, yeah." To be honest, I'd completely forgotten. After I'd met Lloyd, pretty much everything else had gone flying out of my head. I reached into my bag to retrieve the notes Chloe had given me. But trying to recall the helpful tips she'd given me while we'd been at the office wasn't an easy task while inside my old flat's living room and faced with a pair of reporters who I was having increasing second thoughts about letting this deep into my life.

"Are you ready, Robin?" Clarice called to me from the sofa. "I can edit out the background if you like."

"No need." The off-white wallpaper was generic enough for nobody to guess our location.

Speck crouched behind the computer while Clarice patted the seat next to her.

Here we go. I took the remaining seat and placed Chloe's prompting cards on the sofa's arm. Ramsey, meanwhile, angled his armchair away as if to ensure he didn't show up within breathing distance of the camera. I might have found the sight amusing if not for my own nerves.

"Out of interest, where are you going to show the interview?" I asked. "Not the *Blue Moon?*"

"Where else?" said Clarice. "We might not work there anymore, but they'll jump at the chance to feature an exclusive interview with the Head Witch."

I bet they will. "I agreed to protect Lloyd Burton's privacy, but anyone else connected with the story might be in danger. Do you both understand that?"

"Danger?" Speck's eyes rounded. "From your aunt?"

"I assume you weren't working for the *Blue Moon* yet when their office burned down twenty years ago." I didn't wait for an answer. "Never mind. If you're sure you want to take the risk, we'll start."

Speck handed me a microphone, which I took, trying to calm my breathing. *Remember the script.* I picked up the first note card and balanced it at an angle where it wouldn't show on the camera.

Speck turned on the camera, while Clarice flicked her wand and conjured up a pen and notepad. The pen immediately started scribbling on the paper as she launched into her animated, over-the-top interviewer mode.

"We're Clarice and Speck, and we're here with an exclusive interview with Robin Wildwood, Head Witch of Wildwood Heath and the surrounding region!" said Clarice. "This is the first live interview she's offered since she took the title of Head Witch, and I have a feeling this is going to be a *very* revealing discussion. Let's begin!"

The questions were easy to start off with. How was I finding being Head Witch? What did I think of the latest developments in the magical world? Standard stuff. It was only a matter of time, though, before they reached the inevitable.

"We've heard all kinds of rumours out of Wildwood Heath lately," Clarice said in a conspiratorial tone. "Among other things, there's talk of the coven leader stepping down and the Head Witch's leadership being called into question in the wake of an incident involving a demon. Is that true?"

The note card in my peripheral vision wavered before my eyes, and the words went careening straight out of my head. There was zero chance Chloe and I could have anticipated any of this when we'd written the initial plan, and I had no choice but to go off-script.

I looked into the camera. "I'll give you the truth. To be frank, I shouldn't be sharing all of this publicly, but I believe in being honest. I've made a fair few mistakes in my time as Head Witch, but I'd like to think that dishonesty isn't one of them."

I didn't need to see my brother to know he'd be glaring at me for daring to admit to being imperfect, but I had no desire for any more subterfuge. This was too important.

"Please, tell us more!" said Clarice.

"All right." I took in a breath. "The Wildwood Coven was recently attacked by demons. There was no warning. I was able to defeat the monsters using the sceptre, but while my mother was recovering from the attack, my aunt Shannon called the rest of the council together and pressured them into voting her in as the interim coven leader. She then challenged me as Head Witch, on the basis that I didn't inform the rest of the coven before I went to save my family from the demon."

Clarice's mouth hung open. "Your aunt... Shannon Wildwood?"

"Correct," I said. "More crucially, I've also unearthed evidence that Shannon Wildwood was involved in an incident that puts her own competence into question and suggests that her leadership would be a disaster not just for the coven but for the Head Witches as a whole."

"Evidence?" she said in a hushed voice. "What incident?"

"Twenty years ago, Shannon Wildwood's husband had an affair with a prominent member of another coven, the Burdocks." I launched into the journalist's story, laying out the facts. "Shannon found out and confronted him at the coven's headquarters. Unbeknownst to her, the Burdock Coven was dabbling in dangerous magic and had captured a number of demonic creatures. During the fight, the demons broke free of the magic containing them, and Shannon Wildwood fled, locking the coven members into the building alongside her ex-husband. Every single one of them was killed."

Clarice's mouth hung open. She made a faint gasping noise, but not a word escaped, so I pressed on. "Luckily, my grandmother was able to banish the demons, but they're immortal beings that cannot be killed. From their prison in the afterworld, the demons declared revenge on my entire family, and after my grandmother's death, that grudge passed on to the next Head Witch. Me."

A choked noise came from Ramsey's direction. His hands gripped the armchair as if he was trying to restrain himself from jumping across the room and cutting me off, but Clarice and Speck were too busy gawking at me to notice.

"In less than a month, Shannon Wildwood intends to illegally take the sceptre away from me," I continued. "Not to fight the demons but to further her own ambitions. None of her allies have any idea of her history with the

Burdock Coven, nor that one member did survive the attack."

"Who?" Clarice managed to squeak out.

"The daughter of the coven leader, Linnea." I took in a breath. "She blamed the Wildwoods for the deaths of her family members and even went as far as to ally with the demons to take revenge. She was behind the most recent attack, and it's clear that both she and the demons are far more likely to achieve their aims with Shannon wielding the sceptre."

"This... this is true?" she said faintly. At a guess, I wasn't the only one who'd gone off-script.

"Yes." My heart skittered as I looked directly at the camera. "I'd also like to make an appeal to any other Head Witches who might be listening to or reading this interview. I want them to consider what might happen if someone like Shannon Wildwood gained the title of Head Witch. The duty of a Head Witch is to defend her town, not sacrifice others for her own gain. The same goes for a coven leader. Their duty is to their coven, not to themselves."

"The coven leader..." Clarice seemed to pull herself together a little. "You said she claimed the title of coven leader too? Your mother is still recovering from the attack?"

Nice try. "My mother is more than capable of defending her own title, but it's clear that Shannon Wildwood's ambitions are a danger to all of us. The sceptre chose me for a single job: to take my grandmother's place after her untimely death and banish the demons. I intend to do exactly that."

"I think that's all for today," said Clarice breathily. "Thank you, Head Witch."

As the recording stopped, I stood on legs that I hadn't known were shaking and crossed the room to where Ramsey had left the camera on the arm of his chair. "We can watch the footage now if you want more proof."

"Now?" Ramsey sounded hoarse. "You want to watch it now?"

"Wasn't that the plan?" I'd thought he'd brought the camera here precisely because the reporters needed to see proof of my aunt's misdeeds with their own eyes. "I thought we were sharing with a select few people and pretending we got the camera from the local Wardens who recovered it from the scene. Not from Lloyd. I promised him I'd remove all references to him from the story."

"We won't tell anyone," Clarice said quickly, eyeing me with a mixture of awe and fear. "Can we see?"

My brother glared but didn't rise from his seat, so I took that as my cue to go on. It took a few minutes for me to figure out how the old-fashioned camera turned on, and the grainy image that appeared on the screen was difficult to make out at first.

"I think I've done it." I held out the camera so that the others could see the screen when they leaned over my shoulder. "What's that?"

"A wall," said Ramsey.

So it was. To be more precise, the screen showed the wall of a grand old house not unlike our own coven head-quarters, panning upward to a window with the curtains drawn. The camera pressed to the window at the point where the curtains met and a sliver of light poked through, but the room on the other side was cast entirely in darkness.

"How dare you!" Aunt Shannon's shriek made me jump so violently that I nearly dropped the camera. "You dare to make a mockery of me!"

Clarice and Speck both yelped as a horrible noise drowned out her voice, sounding like a cross between some wild animal growling and an inhuman scream from the depths of hell itself. The camera jolted as the person holding it stumbled backwards and the curtains of the downstairs room blew wide.

A gasp caught in my throat. The trembling intensified, and the curtains in the downstairs room billowed outward, revealing the monstrous forms of afterworld monsters hidden within the darkness.

Screaming rang from the house. The camera jerked again, showing a sideways view of the front door opening. A figure ran out of the house, blond hair askew, recognisable as my aunt even from the skewed angle. Such was my shock that I almost missed the moment when she pointed her wand at the door and cast what I assumed was a locking spell.

She turned away, and her wide-eyed gaze connected with mine, as if she was staring straight through the camera lens and into my eyes.

Then she was running, and so was the journalist, muffled screams from the house following in their wake. The camera bounced up and down, no longer showing the house but the street of a town that I might easily have mistaken for Wildwood Heath if I didn't know better.

My finger slipped onto the "off" switch, and the camera dropped into my lap, my heart racing as if I was right there at the scene. "I think we've seen enough."

"That… was Shannon Wildwood," said Clarice.

"It's just as Lloyd described." I wiped my sweaty hands on my cloak. "We aren't going to widely show this footage, but if anyone at the *Blue Moon* has doubts about my story, you can tell them to contact my brother."

"Keep me out of this," said Ramsey. "I said I'd keep the footage myself, not show it to any reporter who calls my office."

"Oh, nobody at the *Blue Moon* will ask," said Clarice, sounding faint. "They'll print the story regardless."

"That's why we need it shared in other places too," I said.

"I want that story everywhere you can get it." Anywhere the other Head Witches might see it. Even in the magical world, the internet was good at spreading information—or *mis*information—and I intended to use that power for good.

"I—yes, but there might be a delay," said Clarice. "We can write up the story and send it to the *Blue Moon* first thing tomorrow, though."

"Good." As for the camera, it'd be safer in Ramsey's hands. If Aunt Shannon did find out we'd been to Lloyd's house and somehow got inside, she wouldn't be able to destroy the evidence she'd failed to obliterate twenty years ago.

Twenty years. She was barely older than I am. And she'd had kids at home... *stop that, Robin.* There was no justifying locking people inside a house full of demons to save her own skin, no matter how terrified she'd looked in the video. And there was certainly no justifying what she'd done to Lloyd either.

Clarice and Speck gathered up their equipment and left the apartment. When we got outside, the reporters departed fast enough to make me suspect they were planning to barricade their doors as soon as they got home and purchase magical cannons or attack hedges like Lloyd had.

"So... there's that." I risked a glance at my brother, whose glower suggested he was preparing to give me an earful. "Too late to turn back now."

"If they print that story, you'll have a target on your back, and so will those reporters."

"I already have one," I said. "Several, in fact. I might also remind you that being dishonest with people is what landed me in this mess in the first place."

"There's a world of difference between informing your council of recent movements and sharing our coven's secrets with the entire magical world."

"And one is considerably more useful than the other," I

countered. "You said yourself that the council has limited power. What does have power, though? Words."

"And this?" He held up Lloyd's camera, which he'd taken for himself. "I'm not showing this footage to anyone who sees your interview and comes nosing around town."

"You don't have to," I said, "but it might be a good idea to save a backup somewhere. You know, in case that thing spontaneously combusts in your storage room."

His jaw tensed. "Shannon shouldn't even know we left town."

"And when she sees the interview?" Were we prepared for the fallout? "Also, we should check she hasn't invoked some other coven law in our absence and made herself supreme lord of the universe or something."

"Yes, we'll go home," he agreed. "And then you and I will have a talk."

"You know what, I'd rather go and talk to the Wardens instead." Not that I'd spared much thought for the other recent development. "You did say they found Leona."

"Yes, but it sounds like they're being careful not to draw attention while they pin down her location," he said. "I gather that they found the general area she's hiding in, but she's moving around a lot."

"I can't believe she's even alive." On top of everything else the past couple of days had thrown at me, Leona's survival wasn't the most surprising development, but still. "I guess we don't need to visit the local Wardens' branch now that we know exactly why Linnea hates our family, do we?"

"No," he said. "We don't."

Aunt Shannon might not have murdered the Burdock Coven herself, but I could easily see how Linnea had pinned the blame on my family in the absence of any other options. And both my aunt *and* Grandma had mutually decided to hide the truth. No wonder Grandma had warned Ramsey when she'd heard I was planning to speak to a journalist. She must have remembered that there'd been a witness.

Did she know Aunt Shannon had threatened him, though? That I couldn't say, but Grandma and I needed to have a chat. Again.

10

Ramsey and I arrived back in Wildwood Heath in the exact spot we'd left from—namely, the middle of the living room. My clone, of course, was no longer here, but I saw the back of Piper's head through the window overlooking the back garden.

When I rapped on the glass, she spun around, gasped, and ran back to the half-open door into the kitchen. "You're back!"

"Yeah." I closed the door and led the way into the living room, where I slumped on the sofa, feeling as exhausted as if I'd run a marathon. "Did my clone behave herself?"

"Oh, yes." Piper joined me. "She walked to the office with your familiar, and if your aunt was watching, she didn't notice anything amiss."

"Let's hope it stays that way." It was barely noon, but I felt like going back to bed. "Tansy's at the coven headquarters?"

"She's been running back and forth between there and the house all day." She rose upright. "I can fetch her."

"I will," Ramsey offered. "I'm going back to work anyway,

and it will look less suspicious for me to drop in at your office."

"You're already going back?" I eyed the camera in his hands. "With that?"

"Yes," he replied. "Did you want me to call the Wardens and set up another meeting?"

"Whatever happened to staying put in Wildwood Heath?"

"I'd go with you, of course."

"Right." An idea hit me. "You know… you might want to ask them to send one of their team members to keep an eye on Lloyd's house. I feel like he'll need the extra protection after the story comes out." Clarice and Speck, too, but I didn't know where they lived.

His jaw tensed. "You really aren't going to change your mind?"

"No, Ramsey, I'm not."

"And the council?" he asked. "Are you going to tell them *before* they see the article?"

"Do any of them read the *Blue Moon*?" He had a point, though. "I guess it's probably a good idea for me to talk to them today so I don't get accused of keeping secrets again."

Not that my aunt was one to talk, given the bombshell she'd been sitting on for the past two decades.

Ramsey sighed and left the house while I watched through a crack in the curtains, putting off the moment when I had to give Piper the gory details. Though telling her would be easier than relaying the same story to Rowan.

Within a few short minutes, my brother returned, approaching the house with someone very familiar behind him. Me. Tansy padded at my clone's side and sprinted into the house when Piper opened the door.

"Finally." She jumped straight at my face in the squirrel equivalent of a bear hug. "Don't you dare leave me behind again."

"Mmf." I sneezed when her tail tickled my nose as she climbed over my face and settled into her usual spot on my shoulder, her tail wrapping around my neck. "It wasn't that bad, was it?"

"Your clone is so *boring*."

I lifted my gaze to where the other Robin stood with her gaze fixed blankly on the wall. "I'll get rid of her."

"And I'll go back to work while you two catch up." Ramsey left the house, while I faced the clone and lifted my sceptre.

Mercifully, my reversal spell worked on the first try, and the clone popped out of existence with the same suddenness with which it had arrived. Being watched by my creepy reflection would have made it even harder to relive my conversation with Lloyd and subsequent interview, though Piper was probably the easiest person to tell. I gave her the details in brief while Tansy ran in circles around the room and occasionally stopped to curse at Aunt Shannon.

"Whoa." Piper sucked in a breath. "You're really going to tell the whole world about the demons?"

"Not the whole world, just the part that reads the *Blue Moon*." And anyone else Clarice and Speck managed to get on board, but that would come later. "My brother's mad at me, but I didn't do this because I *want* my face plastered across every media outlet in the magical world. I want Aunt Shannon gone. This is the only way."

"If you're sure," she said. "You're not going back to work now?"

"I do need to tell Chloe." Rowan first, though. She was far more important, and telling her the truth about her mother's role in her father's death would take all the emotional fortitude I had in me. Paperwork could wait, and so could the council. I was sure all of them except Belinda had stayed at home again anyway, so I opted to walk to the café next.

Rowan had taken the day off so she could help Piper with my alibi and keep an eye out for trouble from her mother's direction.

"She's been quiet," Rowan said to me when I met her at the café. "I think you fooled her. Great job on that cloning spell, by the way."

"Mm." My throat closed up. "I think we should talk upstairs. In your flat."

"All right." She led me up the narrow staircase to the room above the café, which she'd rented out following her expulsion from her mother's house and had turned into a cross between a gaming cave and a terrarium. Tanks of spiders filled one wall, while a large flatscreen TV faced the sofa, equipped with all her gaming consoles. I moved an empty pizza box off the sofa and sat down.

Rowan might have been all too aware of her mother's habit of deception, but the true extent of her lies hit like a blow to the head. She gaped at me, tears flooding her eyes, when I told her how her father had died along with the Burdock Coven. The colour had drained from her face.

"She—" Rowan choked. "I'm going to *kill* her."

"Wait." I caught her arm as she made a lunging motion towards the door. "Wait until tomorrow at the very least. I can't have her finding out about the story before it goes live."

"Right." She fell back onto the sofa and drew her knees up to her chest. "Will it be in the *Blue Moon*?"

"Yeah, and with anyone else Clarice and Speck can get hold of," I replied. "I told them to circulate the story as widely as possible."

She swallowed, closed her eyes, and nodded. "You know anyone involved will be on her hit list."

"Yeah. I've kind of promised to protect the reporters from Aunt Shannon's wrath."

She winced. "I can definitely believe she burned down that guy's house. After what she did to my dad…"

If I'd ever felt the slightest bit sorry for Aunt Shannon when I'd seen the video, my sympathy at her fear thoroughly evaporated at the tears in Rowan's eyes. I pulled her into a hug. "I'm sorry."

"He was a *terrible* dad," she mumbled. "I wasn't even a year old at the time. I don't remember him. Vanessa does, though. Someone should tell her."

"Would even that convince her to leave your mother's side?"

"I guess not." She gave a faint sob. "God, our family's a mess, isn't it?"

"Understatement of the century." I hugged her tighter. "I have until tomorrow morning to prepare to deal with her wrath. I should probably warn the council too."

Rowan wiped her eyes. "Before the story goes out? What if one of them tells her?"

"Good point." I had an inkling I'd have a tough time getting them in to work today regardless. "I'll have them come in to an emergency meeting at the same time as the story is due to go out. That way, she has no advance warning."

"That'd work." She sniffed. "But… you know, if the story goes out, won't they find out you didn't tell them the truth about the demons too?"

"I'm counting on them thinking Aunt Shannon's lies are worse than mine," I admitted. "But yeah… that's an issue."

In the end, stopping Aunt Shannon would be impossible without committing to absolute honesty. I just hoped my tenure as Head Witch would survive the fallout.

———

Morning arrived after a long night of me lying awake staring at the ceiling, and in the end, I had to ask Tansy to take my phone out of the room to stop me from refreshing the *Blue Moon*'s website to see if the article had shown up yet.

Chloe had agreed with my plan to call an emergency council meeting when the article went live. I'd rather have given the others more warning, but that would also have tipped off Aunt Shannon. Like I'd said to Rowan, I couldn't take the risk of her finding a way to erase the article from existence before it reached publication.

No messages arrived from Clarice and Speck while I choked down my breakfast and my brother left for work. I hit refresh one last time as I left the house with Tansy. "Where is it?"

"It isn't nine o'clock yet." She jumped onto my shoulder and flicked my nose with her tail. "Stop worrying."

"Little hard." The meeting was set for nine thirty, and I'd never been so conscious of the ticking clock in the corner of my office when I walked in.

Chloe already sat behind her desk. She might even have slept there, though not much, judging by the oversized bags under her eyes. There was also no sign of Grandma. There hadn't been when I'd come here yesterday afternoon, either, though I'd tried a dozen times to start a conversation with her about her knowledge of the Burdock Coven's fate.

"She isn't here," Chloe said as if guessing my thoughts. "I haven't seen her either, and I've been here an hour."

"I did tell you not to work overtime, didn't I?"

"I thought I'd have another try at disentangling the spell on the phone lines preventing me from reaching the other Head Witches."

"Still no luck?" We'd made a couple of attempts yesterday, but I'd been so exhausted by the time I'd come in to work the following afternoon that I hadn't had the energy to use the sceptre to unravel Aunt Shannon's latest act of trickery. Better to wait until the article went live, in my mind.

"Have you seen any sign of the article yet?" I asked. "I haven't heard from Clarice and Speck."

"No. I hoped you might have."

"It's nine." I'd already set the meeting time, and the others would be arriving soon, but still no article materialised no matter how many times I refreshed the page. I even opened Grandma's old laptop and tried a browser on there in case my phone was the problem.

"Robin, it's not there." Tansy stood on my laptop and blocked my view of the screen. "You should plan what you're going to tell the council instead when they ask why you dragged them into an emergency meeting."

I repeated her words to Chloe, whose expression clouded. "You can tell them the Wardens found Leona. It's true, isn't it?"

"Yes, but what if our unwanted leader shows up?" *Is this her doing?* "You know… I have the interview transcript."

Clarice had sent me a copy, which I'd sent to Chloe and printed out the previous day. I also had a backup saved in case one of my aunt's phone-tangling spells shut down the electricity or the building caught fire.

"You want to hand out the script for them to read?" Tansy asked dubiously.

"Maybe not Wisteria. Her eyesight isn't that great anymore." I looked at Chloe pleadingly. "What did she *do*?"

Ten minutes until the meeting was due to start and still no article. I watched the seconds tick down and dread tightened my chest like a vice.

"Let's go." Chloe beckoned. "Tell them about the Wardens. It'll be fine."

No. It won't, and we both know it.

I carried the sceptre to the council meeting room with as

much trepidation as I'd had while I'd been on trial and took my seat. My brief hopes that the room would remain empty were dashed when the door opened a heartbeat later and Aunt Shannon herself sauntered into the room.

I stiffened in my seat. "What are you doing here?"

"I heard the Head Witch had called a meeting." She gave me a smile. "It's rather unorthodox not to ask the coven leader to attend, isn't it?"

I'd kind of hoped you wouldn't find out until it was already in progress. Not that this was in any way a surprise. If she'd suppressed the article, she hadn't been able to resist the opportunity to gloat.

"Yes," I said. "It is."

Don't give anything away. I gripped the stack of papers— the transcript—which I'd positioned on my lap underneath the desk, while more council members began filing in. Belinda sat down and started knitting. Vanessa, Wisteria, and Janine sat close to their fearless leader. At a guess, one of them had told Aunt Shannon, but Chloe hadn't breathed a word of the actual reason for the meeting to anyone when she'd told them. How had my aunt figured it out?

My suspicions multiplied when she let me start the meeting without objecting.

"We're here for an urgent discussion pertaining to a danger threatening the coven," I began. "That's why I called this meeting."

My aunt made a soft noise of amusement. "Are you here to admit that you knew the demons presented a threat to the coven long before anyone else did?"

So that's her game. She must have told the council that the sceptre had chosen me to banish the demons, and given the accusing stares the others were levelling in my direction, they'd taken it about as well as I'd taken the news myself.

"I'm referring to the incident twenty years ago," I said. "When the—"

Chloe nudged me in the arm, startling me. She'd never interrupted me in a meeting before. "Head Witch... I'm sorry."

She showed me her phone. On the screen was the *Blue Moon's* website, topped with a giant picture of my face.

HEAD WITCH DISGRACED, said the headline.

She didn't.

She had.

The words below merged into a meaningless blur, but I didn't need to read them to know how screwed I was.

"Yes?" Aunt Shannon raised a brow, a smile pulling at her mouth. "You were saying, Head Witch?"

"I was saying..." My nerve faltered, but the weight of the transcript in my lap reminded me that I *did* have proof, even if it hadn't been printed. "I was saying that there was an incident twenty years ago in which our interim coven leader was involved, and that—"

"You knew?" Wisteria interrupted. "You knew that the Head Witch angered a group of dangerous... *demons?*"

"She did," Aunt Shannon said. "She knew that the demons wanted revenge on the former Head Witch for banishing them, but she decided to fight them alone instead of informing the rest of the coven. Then, when her Reaper ally betrayed her, she was dishonest about that, too, even though her mother was the one who paid the price for it."

"Don't you dare blame me for what happened to my mother." The blood surged in my veins, and I rose from my seat, lifting the transcript in one hand. "My Reaper ally was Linnea Burdock, the lone survivor of the demonic attack twenty years ago in which her family was killed when you locked them in the house with a demon."

Aunt Shannon's smile froze. "What on earth are you talking about?"

Vanessa's face was a mirror of her mother's, down to the flash of panic in her eyes when she saw the transcript in my hands.

"I have the entire story here." I held out the papers. "It's backed up in several other places, too, in case my phone mysteriously stops working. I saw direct video footage as well."

I'd promised not to betray Lloyd's identity as the informant. If she hadn't already found him, I'd never knowingly endanger an innocent person to prove a point, but I'd be in real trouble if she asked *where* the video was.

"Videos can be faked," she said. "Especially by someone trained in photography, as I believe you are, Head Witch."

"That's right," Vanessa added a heartbeat later. "She is."

What? I gaped at her for an instant, shocked that she'd have the nerve and even more shocked that it didn't appear to be a surprise to her that I'd seen the video. The impulse seized me to look out the window to see if the police station was on fire, but even she wouldn't have gone that far. Right?

"I can't do that," I said ineffectually. "I'm a photographer, not a video editor. Anyway—"

"This is pitiful." My aunt shook her head. "Very inventive lies, I'll grant you, but the point still stands."

"She also heard the story from a witness." The voice came from none other than Grandma herself, who'd appeared in the middle of the room with her usual lack of subtlety. "Me."

Wisteria jumped out of her seat with a yelp. The others gasped, including Chloe, while Vanessa lurched back from the table so violently that her chair nearly tipped over.

The transcript slipped in my grasp. I saved it by sheer reflex, my eyes fixed on Grandma's ghost hovering above the meeting room table.

"Yes, I know you haven't forgotten I'm here. Even you, Shannon," Grandma added. "I also say that it's in very poor taste for you to interrupt a Head Witch, even a disgraced one."

Thanks for that. Not that I cared much about her barbed comments when she was the only person who could possibly save me from this situation.

Aunt Shannon recovered first. "This is a meeting for current council members, not deceased ones."

"If you read every page of that rule book of yours, it doesn't say I'm excluded," she countered. "It also doesn't say anything about you having authority over a former Head Witch either."

I fought back a surprised laugh, unable to believe this was really happening and wasn't some sleeplessness-induced hallucination.

"Head Witch," Chloe said in faint tones, addressing Grandma. "As a witness… can you tell the council what you saw?"

"I think I'll let the current Head Witch speak first."

Grandma was defending me? The apocalypse was officially nigh. Her sudden arrival had obliterated what was left of my sense of balance, but I scraped the back of my mind for my original plan and cleared my throat.

"Shannon Wildwood caught her former husband having an affair with a member of the Burdock Coven," I said to the council. "Unbeknownst to both of them, the coven was dabbling in demonic magic."

Wisteria made a choked noise and sank back in her seat. Vanessa had gone milky pale, her gaze now on her mother and not on me.

"During the confrontation, the monsters they'd captured escaped," I went on. "Shannon fled, locking the door behind her and leaving the coven and her ex-husband inside the building with two demons and other... entities." Another moan came from Wisteria, but I continued. "The monsters continued to rampage until my grandmother—the Head Witch at the time—arrived to banish them into the deepest level of the afterworld. The demons never forgave her, as we all found out when they attacked Wildwood Heath a short time ago."

"When did you learn this?" Janine spoke in a tremulous voice.

Next to her, Wisteria had sunk so deep into her seat that the crown of her head touched the table.

"Yesterday afternoon," I replied. "I asked Chloe to call an emergency meeting as soon as I got the news and spent the night gathering and preparing the evidence in the event that Shannon Wildwood attempted to discredit me. Since she was stationed as interim coven leader, no phone calls to any other Head Witches have worked on the office phones, and I had good reason to suspect there would be interference in this case too."

"Absurd," Aunt Shannon muttered.

Grandma floated directly through her chair, which was enough to silence even Aunt Shannon. Being touched by a ghost was incredibly unpleasant. I knew all too well.

"I'm not going to place blame for the actual incident with the demons on Shannon Wildwood," I said clearly. "She wasn't the summoner, but she did conceal the truth of her involvement in the attack and in Linnea Burdock's subsequent grudge against the coven. I believe she hid this information from my mother too."

Gasps ensued from the other council members. Aunt Shannon, though, had gone incredibly quiet. Her daughter stared at her in open horror.

"Moreover, she threatened the life and safety of anyone

who tried to investigate the subject," I said. "The office of the *Blue Moon* caught fire on the very same day."

"You dare to accuse me of arson?"

"I didn't accuse you of anything." I addressed the council instead. "Whatever the case, I already have all the proof I need that the challenge to my leadership is false and unjust."

"You don't have the authority to make that call," said Aunt Shannon. "You're under investigation yourself."

"So are you, now," said Belinda, who'd somehow kept knitting throughout the whole meeting. "If this is true, *both* Head Witches deceived the council, and so did the interim coven leader. Do we put everyone on trial now?"

"What about the demons?" Wisteria rose upward, pointing a shaking hand at Grandma. "If she… if you… the demons…"

"It's all right." Janine took her fellow council member's arm and helped her back into her seat. "The former Head Witch will explain."

"Will she now?" Grandma said in a slightly threatening tone.

Uh-oh. I gave her a pointed look. "I believe the former Head Witch knows the demons better than I do, yes."

"She doesn't," said Grandma. "It's rather simple, however. Demons hold grudges for millennia, and those two took issue with my banishing them into a deep corner of the after-world. Since their return to this realm coincided with my losing my title, my replacement was chosen based on her perceived ability to deal with the crisis."

Aunt Shannon made a faint noise of incredulity and shook her head at me. "Do you claim you're capable of protecting anyone in this room from the demon? They know I'm a far better witch than you are."

"They also know you stole money from the coven and sold illegal potions," I pointed out. "*That* was well documented, and I'd like to think the other council members will remember that when weighing up who is most at fault here."

Grandma gave a loud cackle. "Yes, I think some confessions are in order."

I looked to the rest of the council. Wisteria had slid out of her seat altogether and appeared to have passed out. Janine, by contrast, had subtly moved her chair away from Aunt Shannon's, while Laurel didn't meet my eyes.

I guessed it was up to me, then. "I've already given an account of my story. I didn't learn of the demon's existence until after its first attack this summer, and while I did delay reporting to the council, that's hardly grounds for being demoted from my position. I've never claimed to be perfect, but being imperfect is a long way from being a criminal."

"Lies," Aunt Shannon spat. "Poisonous lies."

"Whatever she claims, do any of you think she'll sacrifice herself for your sakes?" I addressed the council at large. "Most of you saw with your own eyes what happened when members of our coven were possessed. It's something no magic can defend against… except for the sceptre."

Silence descended on the table. Nobody would look at Aunt Shannon, even Vanessa.

"Since I'm new to this myself, it's been difficult to figure out how to share the truth with everyone," I added. "I apologise for deceiving you, and I hope you'll give me the chance to try again."

When no response came, Grandma said, "The Head Witch has been honest with you. If I were you, I'd try to be a little more responsive."

"You're taking her side?" Aunt Shannon's voice dripped with disgust. "You'll be disgraced too."

"Out of being disgraced or dead, I'd pick the first option," said Belinda.

"Can we see the footage?" Janine blurted out. "Or… or the interview?"

"I have the transcript." I held it up, and Chloe, with her usual speed, pointed her wand and conjured up enough copies to hand out among the council members. "These aren't the only copies, of course."

Aunt Shannon's gaze followed the pages as they were passed around the table. "You'll regret this."

"Probably, but the demon is a threat to all of us, and I wouldn't trust you with my finances, let alone with the safety of the town."

"Nobody in their right mind would trust you either."

"Maybe not," I acknowledged, "but it's down to the two of us unless the coven leader wakes up."

"That's right," Grandma said in ominous tones. "Choose wisely."

"*Can* she stand up to the demons?" Wisteria whispered, pointing at me.

"Not alone." What the hell. I'd already chosen to be honest. "It's been a long tradition for the Head Witch to stand apart, but I believe that approach does us no favours and that we're far more likely to be able to defeat the demons if we work together. I'm intending to change my approach to involve all of you in the decision-making process. The downside of that is you might not like what I'm doing. I can't make any promises there."

Aunt Shannon made a sceptical noise. I ignored her.

"You'll tell us?" said Janine. "Everything?"

"As much as I can." I faced the table. "Before that, I want to know… if the trial was to be repeated today, who would you offer support to? Which of us should hold the sceptre?"

Belinda spoke up first. "The Head Witch, of course."

"The Head Witch," mumbled Janine.

Laurel jerked her head in agreement, and Wisteria pulled herself into her chair with a whispered, "Yes."

I suppressed a grin. Aunt Shannon was fuming, but I couldn't say I felt sorry for her in the least. She'd earned this.

"I'll give you the chance to read the interview," I said, "but I'm also happy to stay here long enough to answer your questions and see if anyone has suggestions we might implement. What do you think?"

Everyone thought that seemed reasonable. Except Aunt Shannon, who stood up and left the room, followed shortly by her daughter.

Good riddance.

The questioning took all morning, and I was exhausted by the end. I'd probably never talked so much in a council meeting in my life. As much as it pained me to admit it, Mum not being there helped almost as much as Aunt Shannon's absence did. Every word I spoke in front of the coven leader felt like a test, and it had been safer to let her do most of the talking.

But I was coming to realise that it was only now, when she'd been taken out of action, that I felt I had room to stand on my own as Head Witch.

That didn't mean I never screwed up—there were a few times I said things that caused the council members to gasp in shock, and Laurel still wouldn't look me in the eyes properly—but the others were willing to listen and to join in with the conversation about our options for handling the demons. Even Wisteria, though she kept a firm distance from Grandma's ghost and reacted with visible relief when our spectral visitor finally got bored and drifted out of the room.

There was one slightly thorny subject I hadn't gone near yet. Namely, Aunt Shannon's bribery, or blackmail, whatever she'd used to convince the council to turn on me to begin with. When we'd exhausted all the conversation on security measures to keep the demons from getting into the building, I decided to address the giant manticore in the room.

"I know Shannon claimed to be able to defend you all against the demons," I said to the council. "Did she make any other claims? Or... threats?"

There was an awkward pause. Wisteria cleared her throat. "She claimed she was the only person who could protect us and that she had a weapon that could beat the demons."

"She lied," I said. "There isn't one except for the sceptre. Anything else?"

"My sister," Janine blurted. "She's in hospital with a rare disease. Shannon... claimed she could pay for a cure."

"What?" I asked, disarmed. "She offered you money? That would have come directly from the coven's funds, I assume."

Or from selling illegal potions. Both of which were against the law.

Belinda scoffed. "If no magical doctor has found a cure, Shannon certainly can't, no matter how much money she threw at the problem. I *told* you that."

Janine flushed. "I... I'm sorry, Head Witch."

"Thank you for being honest with me." I turned to Laurel next. "And you? What did she offer you?"

"Nothing," Laurel said haughtily. "She convinced me that you'd lead the council into ruin."

"She told all of us that," Wisteria murmured. "She... she also said that having a ghost in the office was dangerous."

"Will she stay on the council?" asked Belinda. "Or are we kicking her out?"

Ah... good question. In truth, I hadn't thought that far ahead. I'd been more fixated on getting my aunt out of my way than on whether she'd face tangible consequences for her crimes, whatever those might be. I'd have to ask my brother. He might have been a stickler for the rules, but we both knew our aunt would have contingency plans to get herself out of any charges we brought against her.

"Let's save that for another meeting," I decided. "Did any of you have other questions?"

Wisteria spoke. "You said you were close to finding the… demon?"

"The Wardens are close," I said. "My brother's in contact with them, and he'll give me an update when they call with news."

I need to talk to him. He must have figured out by now that the article hadn't gone live as planned, and I needed to make sure that camera footage hadn't mysteriously disappeared too.

"Can you trust the Wardens?" asked Janine. "After that Reaper betrayed you?"

A fair question. "I think so. They have no connection to our family. The mistake I made with Linnea was not checking her history, but that information wasn't widely available, as you might have gathered."

As for the Wardens… whether I trusted them or not, I'd committed to joining forces and didn't have a whole lot of other options. It was all very well revealing that Aunt Shannon had no plan, but my own wasn't exactly well defined either. At least the council seemed to accept my explanation, and the meeting came to a close without anyone else storming out of the room.

When we left, I checked my phone. I'd had it set on silent, but Piper, Rowan, and Harvey had all been trying to reach me, no doubt to tell me what I already knew. The one person who *hadn't* been trying to call me was Ramsey, which was mildly concerning.

But Grandma's ghost blocked my path to the front door.

She floated with her arms crossed over her chest, and when I tried to step around her, she all but herded me into the office.

"I can't believe you did that interview!" she said. "You need to call the reporters and ask them to remove the story from consideration immediately."

"Why would I do that?" Once again, I tried to sidestep, but she extended her hands and pushed me backwards. A full-body shudder racked me at her ghostly touch. "Stop that. As a matter of fact, the story *wasn't* printed, and I'd like to find out why."

"So would I," Chloe said. "Have you heard from Clarice and Speck?"

"No." I skimmed through my phone, but I didn't see their names amid the flood of messages and missed calls. "Not them or Ramsey. Listen—"

"What about the rest of our family?" Grandma barred my way out the door. "You might not care for your reputation, but your mother will never forgive you."

"Would she rather I hand over the sceptre?" I asked. "This was the only way to stop Aunt Shannon from snatching my title while Mum's out of action. I'm supposed to be focused on the demons, not on her."

"You aren't ready to face the demons."

"I'll be the judge of that." So much for her having faith in me. "Out of interest, why all the secrecy around Linnea? You could have told me why she hated our family without mentioning that Aunt Shannon was involved in her coven's destruction."

"No explanation I gave would have ever satisfied you," she said. "You're as persistent as those reporters."

"Thanks." I took a step back when she floated towards me again, but she vanished before her ghostly hands made contact.

Chloe gave me a sympathetic look. "I'm proud of you, Robin. Don't listen to the last Head Witch."

The instant the words left her mouth, she looked mildly scandalised with herself, but she didn't take back what she'd said.

"Thanks." I managed a smile. "She might be right. Mum will be angry, but what did she expect me to do?"

She bit her lower lip. "I'd still be careful. Your aunt might not be able to fool the council any longer, but she still has supporters, and I wouldn't be surprised if she's searching the rule book again for more reasons to challenge you. Vanessa too."

"If I were Vanessa, I'd be doing some serious soul-searching." I moved to the door. "Maybe I should ask Ramsey to arrest Aunt Shannon. The blackmail and bribery alone are reason enough."

I understood why he hesitated, of course. Following the law while remaining loyal to the coven was no easy task, and even Mum wouldn't want her sister arrested. She'd also agree with Grandma's insistence that the interview shouldn't appear in print, but that wasn't the point.

"You're going to talk to him now?" she asked.

"I need to check to make sure nothing happened to that footage. He hasn't tried to call me all day." Unlike everyone else. As I began to move towards the door again, my phone buzzed. Harvey. "Hello?"

"Sorry to bug you at work," he said. "I figured you already knew, but I didn't see the article anywhere online."

"I know. I'm on it."

"Are you okay, though?" he asked anxiously. "I couldn't reach your phone all morning."

"I got tied up in a meeting," I replied. "I'll see you later and explain, but it went surprisingly well. For everyone except Aunt Shannon, that is."

"Oh, that's good," he said. "See you at seven?"

"I wouldn't miss it." I ended the call and turned back to Chloe. "I'm off to see my brother."

"I'll hold the fort here," she offered. "Good luck."

I met Tansy at the front door. She jumped on my shoulder and nuzzled my ear. "You have more patience than I realised. I'd have got out of there when the council asked about the demon for the third time, let alone the fortieth."

"I did promise to answer all their questions," I said. "It's nice that they actually listened for once… wait, were you eavesdropping?"

"I chased Myrtle off too," she said. "Just after your aunt went storming out. I wish I'd seen the rest. You have to tell me everything."

I filled her in as we walked to the town's centre. My aunt was nowhere to be seen—sulking at home, no doubt—but I was more concerned with my brother. The police station wasn't on fire, at least, but he'd better have had a good reason for not getting in touch.

I walked in, made for my brother's office, and knocked on the door. He answered a moment later, as unruffled as ever. "Why didn't you tell me?"

"Tell you what?" he said. "That the article never went live? I assumed you saw for yourself."

I swatted at him. "I was worried about you. I half expected this place to be up in flames." Behind him, I spied the camera sitting on the desk.

"Don't be ridiculous," he said. "I expected Aunt Shannon to be at work, and I was trying to find out who she bribed to keep the article quiet."

"Probably the person who owns the *Blue Moon*." I followed him into the office. "What about Lloyd or Clarice and Speck? She didn't threaten them, did she?"

"The Wardens didn't say," he said. "They called me earlier, but I said you were busy."

My heart sank. "Ramsey, I promised to stop her from going after Lloyd. Did you forget?"

"No, I didn't." He exhaled in a sigh. "I never agreed with that article going public, though. I think it's a mistake to bring the details of our family's entanglement with the demons into the open. The entire magical world doesn't need to know."

"I already told the council," I said. "I told them everything and showed them the interview transcript. I had to. Aunt Shannon showed up at the meeting and forced my hand."

His eyes widened a fraction. "They believed you?"

"Yes, because Grandma backed me up. No need to look so shocked."

"Grandma did?" If anything, he looked *more* surprised, though that part had floored me too. "I suppose she did encourage us to go and talk to the journalist, but I can't imagine she wanted that article in print either."

"That's not the point." I pulled out my phone. "If she tracks where we got that information, it'll lead her straight to Lloyd."

Clarice and Speck were prime targets, too, since their names had been attached to the interview.

"The Wardens would have told me if anything was amiss," he said. "They've had someone watching his house since yesterday, which is no easy task when they're watching the demon too."

He's okay. She hadn't gone after him yet… if I assumed no news was good news.

"Why did they call earlier, then?"

"To set up a meeting to discuss the plan for cornering Leona, of course," he replied. "I said I'd let you know."

"I can meet them this afternoon." No time like the present. "If you don't think Aunt Shannon will make a move."

"I think she'll be too busy licking her wounds," Tansy snickered. "I'm *not* staying behind this time."

"I'll let them know."

While he made the call, I went out into the lobby to make a phone call of my own.

"Robin!" Clarice squeaked when she picked up. "I'm sorry! I don't know what happened."

"What do you mean, you don't know?" I asked. "Didn't you send in the interview?"

"Of course I did!" she said. "I don't know what happened to it. The boss told me—"

"The boss was probably bribed by my aunt," I told her. "Or threatened. You might want to fireproof your house."

She made a choked noise. "She… she's Head Witch now?"

"Of course not," I said, a little put out. "I sent her packing, but she's even more hopping mad than before. Listen—you should lie low for a bit."

"I can call the *Blue Moon*!" she said. "I'll find out what happened to the interview right away!"

"If you want to take the risk." I couldn't be in multiple places at once, and poor Lloyd was the one who really needed a bodyguard after the trauma he'd already gone through.

As the call ended, Ramsey reappeared and beckoned me back into his office. "The Wardens are still at the same inn they were staying at. We can head there right away."

A nagging voice in my head told me that it was unwise to go chasing demons after the tumultuous morning I'd already had, but I'd spent entirely too long sitting in a stuffy room. I needed to get outside, and if the Wardens had concrete information on where Leona was hiding, they'd done what nobody in the coven *or* police had achieved in the weeks since she'd fled town.

As we walked out of the police station, I said, "You know, you can always do the obvious and arrest Aunt Shannon for bribing the council."

"What?" He stopped in midstep. "Have you lost your mind?"

"She *did* break the law," I reminded him. "Several times. There's a half dozen reasons to arrest her, and the bribery and threats are the least of them. She should have been prosecuted over the illegal potions already."

"Our mother was clear that the matter was coven business alone," he said through gritted teeth. "I'd prefer to avoid any other reasons to provoke her ire when she wakes up."

"This is about the law, not what Mum wants." This probably wasn't the time for that discussion, so I dropped the subject for the time being.

Once again, we used transportation spells to reach the country lane where the Wardens were staying. Tansy rode on my shoulder and scampered ahead of me into the pub. Three of the Wardens sat at a table near the door, but the werewolf and vampire were both absent from their group. Were they tracking Leona?

Perry waved me over. "Good to see you again, Head Witch. You've really got yourself in a mess, haven't you? I'm impressed."

"Huh?" How much did they know? If the article hadn't gone public, they wouldn't have seen the extent of what I was dealing with, would they?

"Your brother mentioned that you were in a tedious meeting with a bunch of angry old witches," she added. "Personally, I'd rather be hunting the demon."

"That's true." I glanced at Ramsey, but he didn't look

surprised at her comment. "Did my brother tell you anything else?"

"Should he have?" Perry asked. "Being sent to the most secure house I've ever set eyes on to protect the owner from being attacked by some unknown threat was enough to give me the sense that this is highly confidential, but if you want to tell me more...?"

"No," said Ramsey.

"Be nice." I poked him in the arm as I took my seat. Now that I thought about it, he'd have had to give a good reason to send one of them to guard the journalist's house, but the Wardens must have been used to odd requests in their line of work. "Is that where your friends are?"

"Callum is," Tam answered. "Maurice is keeping an eye on the demon. We've been trading shifts."

"Has anyone shown up at that guy's house?"

"No, but I've never seen a security hedge before," said Perry. "A possessed tree, yes, but not a hedge."

"A possessed *tree?*"

"Long story." She glanced at Farley, who'd visibly shuddered. "You didn't say what was threatening the house's owner, but I'm guessing it isn't the demon."

"That's not why we're here," Ramsey interjected. "You know where the demon is? Right now?"

"In theory," said Tam. "Demon attacks aren't always reported as such, especially in cases like this where the demon is trying to lie low."

"Yeah, its host is too sensible to stay in one place for long," added Perry. "We were lost until we found someone who recognised that photo you gave to us."

"Leona." Someone had seen her? "Where was this?"

"North of here," said Perry. "She'd left town not long after, but we sent Maurice after her, and that guy's like a bloodhound."

Leona really survived. It was unusual for demons to spare any of their hosts, let alone a magical dud, but she must have stayed alive by setting her monstrous hitchhiker upon unknowing members of the public instead. Surely, the demon's generosity wouldn't last forever, though. What did a magical dud have to offer a denizen of the afterworld?

"Is Maurice following her right now?" I asked. "You know where he is?"

"No, but he's a vampire, and he can move faster than a demon," said Perry. "All we have to do is give the word, and he'll zip back here, give us the location, and then zoom off to catch up to her again."

That simple? My heart gave a quiver. Once we got Leona's attention, she'd set her sights on Wildwood Heath. "We need to sneak up on her, not go in with all guns blazing."

Perry gave a nod. "Maurice is the stealthiest on our team. Trust me, she won't notice he's there."

"Good," said Ramsey. "I'll gather a team together to back us up."

"What—now?"

"Whenever you give the word," he said. "If we wait too long, we'll risk Leona giving us the slip."

I thought you said I wasn't ready. He must have had faith in the Wardens or else certainty that Leona would be alone this time and not accompanied by a monstrous army.

No. I knew better than to think this would ever be easy.

"Tomorrow?" I suggested. I was unlikely to gain any sudden new demon-slaying abilities overnight, but I'd also have a little time to tell the council the plan. I'd promised to keep them in the loop, after all, and it would have been in poor taste to go charging off so soon after my promise of honesty.

Could I truthfully say that I was capable of beating Leona, though? That, I didn't know.

12

U pon returning to Wildwood Heath, I went back to the witches' headquarters, entered the office, and found Chloe seated at her desk, where I'd left her.

"Is your brother okay?" she asked.

"Yeah, but I'm going to have to call a council meeting again. The Wardens… they found Leona."

She paled. "You're going after her?"

"Tomorrow," I said. "It'd hardly help my promise to keep the council in the loop if I took off chasing demons without telling them, so I'll do that before we leave."

"And… the article?" she said. "It still isn't published. Does your brother know why?"

"No, but I can guess it involved my aunt blackmailing the owner of the *Blue Moon*." I shook my head. "You know, this would be a lot simpler if I could get Ramsey to agree to have Aunt Shannon arrested."

She winced. "Would he do that?"

"Of course not," I replied. "It might not be worth even trying, considering she's an expert at avoiding consequences for her actions. It's always been that way. She hides behind the coven's reputation and will throw everyone else under the bus in the process."

Including me. The article the *Blue Moon* had printed wasn't the first of its kind, but it was a reminder that while some of us knew the truth, nobody outside of Wildwood Heath was any the wiser. Without the real interview exposed, the false story would be all they'd know.

I spied a new stack of documents on my desk that hadn't been there earlier. "What's all this?"

"Ah… Head Witch correspondence," she said apologetically. "It showed up during the meeting."

"Wonderful." I heaved a sigh. "You know, I think I'll just go and fight the demon today and skip the paperwork."

"Don't say that," she said anxiously. "Are you sure you're ready?"

"The Wardens will be with me," I said to her. "They've got a werewolf, a vampire, and two witches on their team." Plus Tam, but I wasn't sure what he was. "And the Head Witches, if we can break that spell on the phone lines."

"I… think I figured out where the origin point is," she said, after a short pause. "I think it's in her office."

"Aunt Shannon's?" Oh boy. "Do you think we can get in there?"

I'd managed it before, when I'd been looking for proof of her illegal potion dealing, but I had my doubts she'd let me make the same mistake twice.

"I don't know for sure," she said. "I've been testing spells that reveal any hidden magic in the building, but they aren't precise enough. I think… maybe if you use the sceptre, it would be easier."

"And cast what, a revealing spell?" That one was simple enough, so I lifted the sceptre and followed the correct motions. My first attempt knocked a stack of papers off the desk, but on my second, a bright shimmering light appeared in the air above the office phone. It looked a little like a shield from a warding spell, and as I watched, shimmering lines radiated outward through the office door.

"It's on the whole building." Chloe moved towards the door and opened it, revealing a similar haze of light spreading across the entire downstairs floor. "And outside, too, I bet. Let's see if it's any stronger upstairs."

She climbed the staircase to the upper level. I followed, slowing as we approached Aunt Shannon's office. Was the light stronger there? I couldn't tell, and if I broke the door open, there was no telling what security measures she'd installed after the last break-in.

Chloe hesitated. "You know… I don't think it's coming from in there after all."

"It isn't?" I squinted. The light didn't seem any stronger around the office door, but outside, it was difficult to know for sure.

"She might have cast the spell outside. That would account for how far it's spread."

"Better check." I followed Chloe back downstairs to the front door and outside. The shimmering haze spread over the street outside and seemed even brighter in the sunlight, and a sharp vibrancy caught my eye, concentrated on a single point farther down the road.

Aunt Shannon's house.

Of course. "Let me guess… she's at home now?"

"Bound to be," Chloe murmured. "If she cast the spell inside her house… I don't think I can undo it."

Aunt Shannon wouldn't take kindly to me blasting inside to take down the spell. Was I willing to take the risk to get hold of the other Head Witches? "I swear, if she gets us killed, I'll come back from the afterworld with a grudge that'll make the demons' look like nothing."

"You can call the other Head Witches from outside town,"

Chloe pointed out. "Her spell won't reach further than Wild-wood Heath."

My shoulders slumped. "Without the real interview in print, they might not be convinced, especially if they saw the substitute. I'll have to see what my brother says."

He was the one who had the video footage, but I doubted he'd consent to showing all the Head Witches even if we'd had time to visit them all. Besides, the Wardens had already agreed to our plan.

Tomorrow, we'd find Leona and banish her demon.

———

Shockingly, I barely slept that night. After hours of tossing and turning, I got out of bed, thoroughly unre-freshed. At least Kimberly's delicious cooked breakfast put some normality into my day, but my brother barely made an appearance before he headed to the office to gather the police to be ready for when the Wardens got in touch.

In the meantime, I was supposed to tell the council that I was going after the demon. No pressure.

"Better hope your aunt doesn't show up again," Tansy remarked as we left the house and walked past Aunt Shan-non's. Because the curtains were drawn, I couldn't tell if she was in. Vanessa too.

"Maybe she's run out of town," I said hopefully. "If she has, I might be able to unravel that spell blocking the Head Witches from the phone lines after all."

"She hasn't." Tansy swept her tail towards the house. "The magpie's been hovering around, but I didn't see anyone leave. Not her or Vanessa."

"Hmm." I had no doubt she'd concocted a new plan overnight, but I didn't have time to dwell on my aunt's scheming when we had a demon to find. With or without the other Head Witches.

When Chloe and I entered the council meeting room, nobody else was present yet, though it was a relief when the first person to show up was Wisteria and not Aunt Shannon. Janine arrived next and then Belinda, but nobody else.

"Anyone know where Laurel is?" I checked the time. The meeting was due to start, and I couldn't say I'd miss her anyway. "We can start without her."

Has she gone back to Aunt Shannon? She'd never been overly enthusiastic about throwing her support behind me, and it wasn't overly surprising. With no time to lose, I moved to the main topic of the day.

"The Wardens hired by the police have successfully located the demon that possessed Leona," I began. "I wanted to discuss our plan with all of you before I took action, as I promised."

Wisteria, predictably, let out a faint scream and then covered her mouth. "You *found* it?"

"The Wardens pinned down its general location," I clarified. "We haven't drawn the demon's attention yet, but our intention is to make a move today, before the creature realises it's being followed. I'll be joining the Wardens myself. Do any of you have suggestions or objections?"

Wisteria went milky pale. "Is the demon near Wildwood Heath?"

"Not that I'm aware of," I said. "Our aim is to banish it before it can get near the town. The police will be ready if it does, and the town's surrounded by a sage barrier, so you'll be safe here."

Nobody said a word, but the council members' faces displayed varying degrees of panic. Unease trickled down my spine. Should I have told the council at all? There was little they could contribute to the discussion. All of them were far past their demon-hunting prime, if they'd ever had one at all, but I'd made a promise to keep them in the loop.

The door creaked inward, and Aunt Shannon walked in. "Sorry I'm late. I was unavoidably detained."

Oh no. What was she up to this time? "I thought you weren't coming."

"I'm an active council member and the interim coven leader, am I not?"

"Vanessa is an active council member too." So was Laurel, and neither had come with her.

"Yes, but she's not well, poor thing." She strode over to the table and took a seat. "What have I missed?"

Fine. I'll play her game. "We've located the demon, and we're looking for volunteers to help hunt it down. Would you be willing to join me?"

Chloe gave me an alarmed look. For an instant, I wondered if I'd gone too far, but Aunt Shannon merely returned my smile. "I'm afraid that recent events have taught me that hunting demons is not in my area of expertise, but I wish you the best of luck in fulfilling your mission, Head Witch."

My suspicions boomed like one of Mum's quick-flowering plants. *Does she want me out of town?* My guess was *yes,* but I couldn't leave the Wardens to hunt the demon alone.

"Thank you," I said. "Might you have any idea where Laurel is?"

"I really couldn't say."

Couldn't… or wouldn't? Had she employed blackmail or threats again, or had Laurel made up her own mind? More to the point, why had Shannon come back here, and into a room where she was outnumbered? *She has some angle, but she won't tell me what it is.*

"Fine," I said. "There's one small matter I'd like to discuss before I close out the meeting. None of the other region's

Head Witches seem to be reachable by phone. Has anyone else noticed?"

Aunt Shannon's smile widened. "I would assume they're occupied. Most Head Witches have busy schedules, after all."

I ignored the jab. "If the demons *do* find their way to Wildwood Heath, I'm sure the citizens of the town would appreciate the help of the other more powerful witches in the region."

My aunt remained unmoved. "Yes, I expect they would."

Damn her. As much as I wanted to know what she was up to, I didn't need her wasting my time when I had a demon to track down.

"Are there any other subjects that you want to discuss?" I asked the council.

I half expected my aunt to have some absurd diversion, but she didn't, and when I called the meeting to a close, she left the room along with the others.

I lingered in the room to see if she'd set up a booby trap or something, but nothing appeared to be out of place.

"What do you think she was up to?" I asked Chloe when we were back in the office. "Why'd she only show up for the very end of the meeting? Was she trying to prove that we haven't beaten her yet?"

"Might be," she said doubtfully. "Her daughter's not here."

"And Laurel." Her absence was suspicious, but Vanessa was the one most likely to be running dodgy errands on her mother's behalf. "I can send Tansy to look and see if Vanessa is really bedridden with flu."

"Aren't you and your brother meeting the Wardens?"

"He said he'd contact me when they got in touch." No missed calls showed on my phone this time, but the meeting had taken less than an hour. "I might check in with him early. See if the police are prepared."

As little as I wanted to hasten my confrontation with the

demons, staying in the office to wait was even less appealing. No sense in delaying the inevitable.

I went outside to look for Tansy first and found her stalking a pigeon near the flowerbeds in the back garden.

"Hey." I beckoned to her. "We're leaving."

She turned her back on the dim-witted bird, which squawked and took flight at my approach. "The meeting's already done?"

"Yeah, but Laurel never showed up, and neither did Vanessa. Aunt Shannon just came to gloat."

"She didn't, did she?" Her tail twitched. "What's she up to?"

"That's what I'd like to know," I said. "Can you follow her? She might not have left the office yet. I'm going to see if my brother's heard from the Wardens."

"You'd better not go after the demons without me." She scampered off while I left the coven headquarters behind.

When I walked into the police station, Seth, the officer who I sometimes played Pokémon Go with, gave me a wave. "I haven't seen you in a while, Robin. Your brother's kept us busy patrolling the forest."

"Yeah, I can imagine," I said. "Did he tell you…?"

"Oh, yeah, I'm on his team of demon hunters." He ran a hand over his buzzed hair. "Not that keen on the idea, to tell you the truth, but I volunteered. I know what it feels like to… you know."

"Be possessed." I spoke quietly. "I guess people aren't exactly lining up to volunteer."

"No. He had real trouble getting the officers to sign up," said Seth. "In the end, he dispatched a couple of teams into the forest to set up a protective shielding spell around the whole town while they're laying down the sage barrier. You don't need us to come with you, though?"

"No… I think Wildwood Heath needs the protection."

Not just from the demons but from my aunt's scheming. No shielding spell would keep *her* out, and I wondered how much he and the other officers knew about her threat to my leadership. My brother had been tight-lipped, no doubt, and the demon was the priority. While the team had been patrolling the forest and maintaining the sage barrier for weeks, that wasn't the same as the actual monster making another appearance.

"All right." He nodded to my brother's office. "He's in there."

My heart gave a pang. Seth was a good guy. I really hoped the demon didn't come back and hurt him again.

When I knocked, Ramsey opened the door. "I haven't heard from the Wardens yet. Is the meeting already over?"

"Pretty much," I said. "Aunt Shannon showed up to gloat a bit and then left. I don't know what her angle was, but she seemed awfully pleased to hear I was leaving town to fight the demon."

"You shouldn't have told her that."

"I'd already told the rest of the council. Besides, Laurel never showed up, and neither did Vanessa," I said. "Her mother claimed she had flu, but I think we both know that's nonsense. Anyway, I never expected them to help with the demon, but you know, I promised to be transparent with the council."

"Until we hear from the Wardens, we can't go after the demon," he said. "Not without backup."

"Speaking of backup, Chloe still can't get hold of the other Head Witches," I said. "Aunt Shannon cast an enchantment to prevent any phones from reaching them, and Chloe and I figured out the spell's centred on her house."

"Is it?" he asked. "What do you expect me to do about that?"

I blinked. "I mean, you're the head of the police. If anyone has the authority to barge into her house, it's you."

He sighed. "Robin—"

My phone buzzed. I fished it out of my pocket, and the word *Ugh* flitted across the screen.

"Robin!" Clarice's panicked voice squeaked in my ear. "Ah! There's something attacking my house!"

"What?" *Oh no.* "What is it?"

"I don't know!" I heard Speck yelling behind her too. "We can't get out. Please help!"

The call cut out. Adrenaline flooded my nerves. "Ramsey—I think Aunt Shannon attacked Clarice and Speck."

"Don't be ridiculous."

"*Something* is attacking their house." Who else could be responsible? "Are the Wardens still watching Lloyd's house too?"

"They should be."

A monster? What did she set loose on them?

Wait. Who was the best at handling monsters? "Can you call the Wardens and say it's urgent?"

"Robin, they're supposed to be hunting the demon."

"I know you aren't a big fan of Clarice and Speck, but we can't let them get killed." Another possibility hit me. "What if it *is* the demon? If it figured out the Wardens were watching them and traced it back to me..."

I didn't know why they'd have gone after the reporters first, but unlike Wildwood Heath, Clarice and Speck's home wouldn't be surrounded by a protective circle of sage. And the demons had long memories. Had they worked out I'd been probing into the history of their grudge against my family?

Ramsey sighed. "I'll call them."

Poor Clarice and Speck. While he made the call, I left the police station and crossed the street to the café. I hadn't checked on Rowan since I'd dropped the bombshell about her parents on her, so I ducked inside and spied her slumped at a table in the corner over a latte.

"Rowan?" I walked over. "You okay?"

"Definitely not," she mumbled. "Wait, shouldn't you be at work?"

"Got out early. I'm going demon hunting."

Her head snapped upward. "What? Now?"

"Might have to take a detour on the way." I'd told her about the article failing to go up online but not all the details of her mother's more recent treachery. "Clarice and Speck called me, saying some*thing* was trying to break into their house. Not sure if it's related to the demons or your mother's attempt at revenge."

She winced. "Not again."

"I know." I looked towards the door, instinctively, though of course, my familiar wasn't here. "Can you do me a favour? Tansy is over at your mother's house. I need her to come and find me."

"She's at my mum's house?"

"Looking for Vanessa, who never showed up at work," I explained. "Allegedly, she has flu, but I doubt it."

Conflicted emotions flitted across her face. "All right, but... you know she probably wants you to leave town, right?"

I know. "I can't help it. The police are staying behind. It'll just be me and the Wardens hunting the demons."

She got to her feet. "That doesn't seem wise. I know the Wardens are professionals, but..."

"Yeah." No help for it, though.

After we parted ways, I headed back to the police station and found Ramsey outside his office door. "Robin, where did you just go?"

"I asked Rowan to fetch Tansy. You got through to the Wardens?"

"Maurice has gone missing," he said. "The others think the demon caught him spying, and now, they've both disappeared."

I swore. "Leona's gone too?"

He inclined his head. "At a guess, she'll be on her way here."

My heart dropped like a stone. I couldn't ask them to abandon a teammate… but could I save Clarice and Speck without their help? "That means we'll have to bring them here first. The Wardens."

It also meant he'd have to go back on his plan to avoid inviting outsiders to town, but if we wanted to stop Leona, we didn't have a choice in the matter.

"Fine," he relented. "They'll have to come in on foot, though. I had my team set up a shield around town so nobody can use transportation spells to get in and out, in case Leona tries to use one as a workaround."

Good idea. Unfortunately. "Then I hope Clarice and Speck can hang on a little longer."

13

According to my brother, the shielding spell covered the town's limits but ended a short distance into the Wildwood. Ramsey and I met Tansy on the way, accompanied by a steely-eyed Rowan.

"I'll watch my mother's house while you're gone," she offered. "See if she tries anything else."

"Be careful," I warned. "We won't be long, but that shielding spell will slow us down if we need to come back to help."

She gave me a grim smile. "Don't forget it'll stop *her* from getting out too."

"Fair point." I hurried after my brother, who'd strode away towards the forest. "Slow down."

"I thought it was urgent." He continued, entering the Wildwood via the path near our house, and Tansy and I hurried to keep up with him. I didn't see the shielding spell until we were outside of it, a shimmering haze that spread from the forest path as far as the eye could see.

Once on the other side, Tansy jumped onto my shoulder, and Ramsey and I cast transportation spells. We landed on the country lane, where Perry and the others stood waiting outside the pub.

"There's a problem," I said before anyone else could speak. "Clarice and Speck are being attacked by some kind of monster."

Perry's brows shot up. "Well, monsters are usually our thing, but… who are Clarice and Speck again?"

"The reporters who did the story that… never mind." I backtracked. "I'm going to have to go and help them first, but I'll come back and—"

"What?" Ramsey said. "No. The plan was to bring the Wardens to Wildwood Heath and stop Leona from getting in."

"What if this is Leona's doing?" I asked. "The timing is suspicious, and Clarice definitely said some*thing* was attacking them."

"I don't like coincidences either," said Perry. "Tell you what, I can help you deal with that while the others go after the demon."

"No," Tam said. "We can't split up again. We're already missing one team member."

"What's attacking those reporters can't be worse than a demon," she said. "If it is, I'll give you a call."

"I want to check Lloyd's house first," I added. "I just… have a bad feeling he might have been targeted too."

"Is that the other house we were watching?" Perry asked. "Sure, I can do that."

Tam's jaw tensed. "I don't like this."

"Neither do I," Ramsey put in.

"There. You two have a lot more in common than you'd like to admit," I said to them. "We'll be two minutes."

"That's right." With a grin, Perry lifted her wand, and I did the same with the sceptre.

In a flash, we landed outside the journalist's house, which

was as heavily fortified as ever. Perry raised an eyebrow at the closed gates and spiky hedges. "I don't think any monsters have got in there, somehow."

"I just wanted to check," I said. "The guy has reason enough to be paranoid already."

"Because of your aunt?" When I gave her a sideways look, she added, "Come on, I can add two and two. I can also keep a secret. If someone's trying to avoid the paranormal world, they have good reason."

"Yeah." I couldn't see past the gates, and when I moved closer to the hedge, the leaves shifted, branches extending towards me. "Watch out for those."

"Tricky." Perry pointed her wand at the hedge. "Can that sceptre of yours take down the barriers?"

"Yes, but it might blow up the house too." In response to another raised eyebrow from her, I added, "It's not made for subtlety."

"He's inside," Tansy announced from her perch on my shoulder. "I can see movement in there."

"He's okay?" *At least that's one less person to worry about... for now.* "Right. We need to get to Clarice's house... which I've never been to."

"Clarice who?"

"Not sure." I pulled out my phone and loaded the *Blue Moon*'s website. If my instincts were right, she'd be easy to find.

Unlike Lloyd, Clarice and Speck's address was attached to pretty much every article they'd published, and it took one quick search to pull up a picture. Really, it was a wonder nobody had ever tried to burn *their* house down.

I'd have to hope my sceptre was enough to amplify my mental image of the picture that came up in the search. Peering over my shoulder, Perry got out her own phone, which was vibrating with a message. "The others are worried about me. Honestly, it's not my fault Maurice got himself captured."

"How did the demon spot him?" I put my phone away, keeping the image of the house in my mind's eye.

"Vampires can't sense demons. I have no idea," she said. "Maybe he was careless. Ready?"

"I hope so." I shifted position so she could grab my arm and ride tandem. "You should know, I'm going to a place I've never been, so I might transport us onto the roof or something. Fair warning."

"Don't worry. Some of Farley's transportation spells have been far worse," said Perry. "There's a reason I'm usually in charge instead. Let's go."

I lifted the sceptre and pictured the image in the photo, and we vanished in a flash of purple light.

This time, the street we landed on couldn't have been more obviously paranormal if it tried. The trees lining the road were bright pink, for a start, and shed glitter instead of leaves. The houses were widely spaced and large enough to make me wonder just how much working for the *Blue Moon* paid. Each had some kind of adornment, some covered in murals of shimmering paint that changed colours in the shifting sunlight and others topped with roofs shaped like pointy hats or lawns covered in life-sized troll statues instead of garden gnomes.

"This place can't get many non-paranormal tourists," Perry remarked. "Which house is it?"

A loud scream rang out.

"I think it's that way."

I ran in the direction of the noise, spying a house decked out in what appeared to be pages from a newspaper plastered over the bricks. *Yeah, that's the place.*

More screaming. I lifted the sceptre, and this time, I didn't hesitate before pointing it at the door, which flew wide open with a crack that suggested someone would have to cast a repair spell later.

Perry and I ran up to the doorstep and skidded to a halt. The hallway was covered in a sticky weblike substance that looked suspiciously like the net I'd once unearthed in my aunt's garden. An open door on the right revealed a living room equally draped in webbing and two terrified figures pinned to the sofa. Clarice and Speck.

"Head Witch!" Clarice shrieked. "Watch out!"

A growl was my only warning before a giant paw slammed down beside me, turning from transparency to solidity before my eyes. I whipped around, spying dark eyes, slavering teeth, and a long, shaggy coat that was semitransparent at the edges.

I backed up a step, lifting the sceptre. "Ah. So that's what was trying to get into the house."

"That," said Perry, "is a monster. Not one I've seen before either."

"It's a ghast." Aka, one of the few beasties that could outdo a Head Witch. *We're in trouble.*

The beast swiped a paw, gouging into the webbing over the sofa. Based on the marks already present, the sticky webs might well have spared Clarice and Speck from being mauled to death, but they also prevented the pair from fleeing. I stumbled back another step, and my feet stuck fast. *Ack.*

"I'll call backup!" Perry held her phone in her other hand while she waved her wand, sending a wave of something flying upward from her pocket and into the creature's pitted eyes. It recoiled—she'd thrown sage, I guessed—but recovered fast.

As it lunged again, I lifted the sceptre upward and cast a freezing charm. Experience told me it wouldn't last longer than a second, but it won me time to dig in my pocket for my own sage supply—aided by Tansy, who grabbed a bag of sage in her mouth too.

When she flung the sage in its direction, the beast vanished in a swirl of darkness. Into the afterworld. I held my breath, but it didn't reappear.

"Hiding, is it?" Perry pointed her wand at the spot where the monster had vanished. "I guess it's as scared of sage as any other afterworld monster."

"Yes, but it takes multiple Head Witches to banish one. Or a Reaper." Neither of which we had with us.

"Damn." Perry whistled. "I've read about them in the Wardens' notes, but I didn't know they were that lethal. Did that demon call its friends, do you think?"

"Must have." The last person to summon a ghast had been Tiffany Henbane, Leona's former mentor. "Why come here, though? It's not as if it could have followed my trail."

Someone had ordered it to attack the reporters. Why? Clarice and Speck didn't look injured, as far as I could see beneath the sticky webs pinning them to the sofa. They gaped at me, too stunned to move.

"I think the monster's gone," I told them. "We'll get you out of there."

I figured a reversal spell would do the job. I lifted the sceptre and pointed at the sticky webs, and in a flash of purple light, webbing flew everywhere. The sofa rose and fell with such a crash that Clarice and Speck both yelled aloud as they slid onto the carpet. Tansy yelped, too, clinging to my shoulder.

"Watch out!" she squeaked in my ear. "You almost blew my fur off."

"Sorry!" I lowered the sceptre. "Might've been a bit much."

"Th-thank you, Head Witch," Clarice gasped. "What—*was* that thing?"

"It was after me." Of that, I was certain. "I don't think my aunt summoned it either. Did you see where it came from?"

Speck shook his head, while Clarice whimpered, "It came from outside. Are you sure... are you sure it wasn't your aunt?"

"Fairly sure, but the sticky trap was definitely hers," I replied. "If I were you, I'd get out of town for a bit."

My aunt had wanted me to come here, certainly, but even she wouldn't be vindictive enough to set a ghast loose amongst a bunch of innocent people. *I think.* Either way, I was the target, and as long as I remained here, everyone in the vicinity was in danger.

With that in mind, Perry and I left the reporters to clean up the mess of their house and found no traces of the beast remaining outside.

"I think it went back to its summoner." I wished Maura was here. Her ability to sense the afterworld would have enabled her to track the monster's direction—and whether Leona was nearby.

"Yeah." Perry swore. "We'd better get back to my team. I bet they got lost trying to find their way here."

We transported ourselves back to the country lane, where Callum and Farley both ran towards Perry.

"Are you all right?" Callum asked. "Why'd you go off alone? You know none of us can use transportation spells. Robin's brother left too."

"What?" Had he taken off and left me to face the monster? "Did something happen at home?"

"We were fine, thanks to her." Perry gestured to my scep- tre. "The monster fled into the afterworld."

"I was the target." I grew more sure of that the more I thought about it. "I need to go to Wildwood Heath. I can try to bring you with me, but I haven't tried a transportation spell on this many people before."

"Her sceptre is pretty hardcore," Perry added. "She nearly blew the reporters' living room up."

"Did you see Maurice?" she asked. "Or—did the monster…?" She trailed off, her expression stricken.

"I didn't see him, but vampires are hard to kill," Perry said. "Don't look at me like that, Tam. You know it's true."

"It's got to be Leona," I told them. "Her mentor and coven leader sent the same sort of monster after me before. Ghasts… they're powerful enough to kill even a Head Witch."

"That's just bloody perfect," Perry muttered. "Where are the local Wardens when we need them?"

"I've given them a call, but it's hard for them to dispatch a team when we don't know the location." Tam eyed me seriously. "If you're certain it's your home that's the target, that's where we'll go."

"All right." I lifted the sceptre. "Brace yourselves."

Tansy dug her claws into my shoulder, and the others gathered around me as I waved the sceptre, picturing home. A flash of purple light engulfed us, the world lurched sideways, and instead of landing on the street as I'd intended, I found myself lying flat on my back on a muddy hill, with Tansy still clinging to me.

"Ow." Next to me, Perry lifted her head. "Do you have a shielding spell around your home, by any chance?"

"I forgot." I winced as Tansy relinquished her grip on my shoulder. "Ow. That hurt, Tansy."

"I didn't want to end up being pitched halfway across the Wildwood," she retorted. "That was *horrible*."

"Is your familiar talking to you?" Farley sat up too.

"Yeah… my coven's gift is speaking to animals." I rose to my feet. "Sorry. We'll have to enter the town on foot."

I took off at a run downhill, ducking through the

entrance to the woods and weaving down well-trodden paths until I came to the road leading to the coven's head-quarters.

There, Ramsey strode to meet me. "Robin—come with me."

"Did you forget your shielding spell locked me out?" I said breathlessly. "Why did you take off and leave me and Perry to fight the monster alone?"

"Our mother is awake."

My attention snapped over to the house, from which he'd emerged. "She's what?"

Tansy jumped off my shoulder, but I remained rooted to the spot for an instant. *She's awake? Now?*

"The Wardens... I brought the Wardens with me."

Ramsey didn't appear to even hear me. "Our mother is still somewhat disorientated, but she's well."

A gasp lodged in my throat. My legs started working again, and I ran, behind my brother, into the house and up the staircase. Through the open door, Mum peered out from where she sat up in bed. Horace, her familiar, lay across her legs in a way that suggested he was making a concerted effort to stop her from getting up.

"Mum," I whispered. If we'd been the sort of mother and daughter who hugged regularly, I'd have done so, but her murderous expression was more that of an angry coven leader than a loving parent.

"Robin," she said, "what *have* you done?"

Where to even start? "You... are you okay?"

"Obviously," she said tersely. "My mother told me that you were busy upending the coven headquarters when I was gone."

"You..." My thoughts tripped over themselves as I tried to arrange them into some kind of coherent order. "Did she tell you your sister stole your position and tried to steal mine too?"

"She told me that Shannon attempted a coup, yes," she said. "And in retaliation, you called the press and exposed our family's secrets for the world to hear, turned the council into your personal committee, and went to hunt the demons alone. Do I have that right?"

My mouth fell open. "That is not how it happened."

Grandma had told her that? I should have known that as soon as Mum woke up, the former Head Witch would abandon her brief foray into supportiveness, but the sheer whiplash left me gaping.

"Really?" She raised a brow. "You'll have plenty of time to enlighten me later, but as my familiar keeps reminding me, I need to take things slowly to avoid hampering my recovery."

"We don't have time." Dread cascaded over me. "There's a ghost chasing me, and Leona, too, and—" I broke off as Mum made to get out of bed, only to be thwarted by her familiar.

"Stay put," he told her. "The town is surrounded by sage *and* a shielding spell. Whatever you've managed to draw to our doorstep will be unable to enter the town."

"There's…" The Wardens were outside. Someone needed to give them direction, to help them find their missing teammate, but indecision left me paralysed. "That doesn't mean they won't try. A ghost is impossible for me to banish alone, and—and your sister has set up a spell preventing anyone from calling the other Head Witches. Did Grandma mention that part? Or that she bribed and threatened the other council members?"

"So you thought telling the press would help?" Mum enquired.

"The story never even went out!" I turned away, my eyes stinging with tears of frustration. "If you knew what she did twenty years ago—wait, *did* you know?" I whipped back to face her.

Her expression remained impassive. "Are you referring to the incident with the Burdock Coven?"

I took a step back, into the doorway. "You—*knew?* Like Grandma? You knew why Linnea wanted us dead?"

"Not that, no," she replied. "My mother only told me Linnea's connection to the Burdocks when I woke up. I did know the demons killed them."

"Because Shannon *locked* them in the same house as a group of monsters." My voice trembled. "She threatened that journalist—he's been living in terror of retaliation for twenty years. How can you think that's okay?"

"I didn't know about any journalist," she said. "There's no need to look at me like that, Robin. My sister's tactics are well known, and while I'm aware that she took advantage of my absence, you shouldn't have allowed her to push you."

"I didn't know when you would wake up, did I?" Tears scalded my cheeks. "I didn't know if you *would* wake up. Your sister would never have fought the demon. She'd have sacrificed everyone else first, including me."

"There was no need to provoke Leona this soon," she said. "There was certainly no reason to tell the council and instigate a panic."

"Your sister is the one who told them." Nice of Grandma to enlighten her on that. "She told them everything about the demon's grudge against our family and convinced them she alone had the means of protecting them. She was able to get away with lying precisely because nobody tells anyone anything. I realise that keeping secrets is second nature to you, but that's exactly what Aunt Shannon used in her accusation against me. Maybe we don't need that approach anymore."

Mum took in a breath. "I'm going to get dressed. I'll talk to you later, Robin."

Tansy nudged my ankle, urging me out of the room, and she jumped up to my shoulder as I walked out. "I'm sorry, Robin."

"She hasn't changed a bit." I rubbed my eyes with the back of my hand as I walked away from the room. *How can this have gone so wrong?*

"Don't forget the Wardens are waiting outside," Tansy reminded me. "Or they were."

Through the open door, I saw my brother standing outside but no sign of the Wardens. "Where are the others?"

"I sent them away," he said.

"You did *what?*" As my voice rose, birds circled overhead, joining the ones already massing above the house in response to my churning emotions. I took in a couple of breaths in an attempt to calm down. "Why did you send away the people who came to help us?"

"This is not an appropriate time to have visitors."

"Did you not hear me saying a ghost is chasing me, as well as the demon—who, I might add, has captured one of the Wardens' teammates."

"Clearly, the demon isn't here, and neither is their teammate."

I bristled. "Just because Mum is awake, it doesn't mean you need to drop everything and obey her every command when she doesn't have a clue what's going on."

"That's not the problem, Robin. Calm down."

"You still think of her as Head Witch and not me, don't you?" That was the crux of the problem. He might have claimed otherwise, but in the end, she'd always hold the authority. "You know, I'm glad I'll be out of here when this is all over, one way or another. None of you ever really believed I could do this."

"Robin!" Chloe came running towards us from the coven headquarters. "I thought I heard your voice. Your aunt... I just saw her and Vanessa fleeing into the forest. I think they're leaving town."

14

Aunt Shannon had gone? "The shielding spell stopped her from using a transportation spell to escape. Pity for her."

That meant we could theoretically catch up if we wanted to, but we'd be better off without them.

On the other hand, if they happened to run into Leona or one of her monsters on the way, there was a strong chance Aunt Shannon would divert them to Wildwood Heath the same way she'd locked the Burdock Coven inside the house to save her own skin. Could I take the risk?

Chloe watched me with concern. "What's going on? Is the coven leader really awake?"

"Yeah." My attention snagged on Aunt Shannon's house. "Wait. That spell binding the phone lines… have you tried calling the Head Witches since she left?"

"No…" Chloe gasped when I ran towards the door. "You can't break into her house."

"There's a ghast on its way here," I said over my shoulder, "and my brother just helpfully sent away the people who were supposed to help defend us. Also, I can hardly fall any lower in Mum's esteem. According to her, I should have laid down and let Aunt Shannon take over while she was unconscious, but if I had, that would have been my fault too."

Sparks flew from my sceptre in response to my anger, leaving sizzling holes in Aunt Shannon's hedge. *Oops.*

"I'm sure that's not what she meant." Chloe hesitated behind me. "There are heavy wards on the house."

"Yes, but I have this." I held up the sceptre, having little doubt that even Aunt Shannon's steeliest defences couldn't block its magic, especially when she wasn't around. "Let's see what she's been hiding."

I waved the sceptre and cast an unlocking charm on the front door. Purple light flared to the sky, and I shielded my eyes with my free hand against the glare as the spell rippled outward. A gust of wind slammed into Aunt Shannon's house and blew all the windows open at once, and the sound of a dozen clicking noises warned me that I'd unintentionally unlocked half the doors in the neighbourhood as well.

I lowered my hand. Aunt Shannon's door lay open, but a familiar sticky webbing covered the hallway inside.

"A parting gift. How nice of her."

Tansy padded on my heels, sniffed, and then jumped back with a yelp as a net came flying out of nowhere, splaying on the ground in front of me like a giant spiderweb.

"Careful!" I beckoned my familiar to stay back in case of more traps and lifted the sceptre upward again. "I'll use a revealing spell. Should've done that from the start, really."

I wasn't thinking straight. My conflicted emotions continued to rage, causing birds to circle above my head and the occasional spark to fly from the sceptre's end. Treading carefully in case of any other falling nets, I cast a revealing spell.

Light bloomed from the sceptre, bathing the house in vibrant purple—especially the area around the door.

"I don't think it's safe to go through there." Tansy edged closer to the house, angling towards the living room window. "Hey… what's in there?"

The glow came from a point to the right-hand side of the window, but treading closer meant navigating a minefield of other booby traps. Tansy, being smaller, was able to skirt the traps faster and peered in through the window.

"Oh, look at this," Tansy said. "It's a very complicated contraption made out of mirrors covered in warding spells."

"What's that?"

"What's what?" Chloe asked from her safe vantage point outside the gate. "Has she found the spell blocking the landlines?"

"Something involving mirrors and warding spells." Magic and technology didn't always go together, but some had found innovative ways to merge spells with modern conveniences, and unlike the rest of the council, my aunt couldn't be said to be behind the times.

"A deflection spell," she said. "Is there a phone in the middle of the contraption? I wondered if she might be doing something like that. Anyone who tries to call will find their signal… erm, bounces off the mirrors. It's very tricky magic, and I'm not sure I entirely understand it."

"Nothing's too tricky for her," I muttered. "Would I have to go inside to break it?"

"Not if I chew through the cables," Tansy said. "I can get in through the window."

"No way," I protested. "You can't see any hidden booby traps."

"I can smell them," she said. "And your glowing light is everywhere. Hard to miss."

True. The house glowed like a neon disco party, and to take out all the security spells would require some serious work with the sceptre that might well knock her entire house over in the process. While I didn't much care about destroying her property, there might be evidence of other misdeeds hidden in there too. Evidence I'd need later.

"Fine," I relented. "But please be careful."

"My eyes and ears are open." Tansy scaled the wall and squeezed through the squirrel-sized gap in the window, landing lithely in the room on the other side. "Wow, you unlocked every drawer and cupboard in here too."

"Don't get distracted." I heard rustling then a muffled, *aha!* "Found the spell?"

"Yes," she said in a muffled voice. "No cables are a match for my teeth."

"Don't electrocute yourself." I listened, waiting for Tansy's reappearance, and heard more thuds and crashes. "You okay?"

"Yes. There are some *weird* potions in here."

"More souvenirs from the Henbanes?" If Ramsey hadn't gone back to the police station, I'd have been able to send him in there to confiscate them, but we had more pressing issues at hand. "Come out, and I'll seal the place up so she can't remove any evidence before we call the police."

When Tansy's lithe squirrel form came sliding out the window and down to the ground, I pointed the sceptre at the window and cast a locking charm.

"Robin!" Mum stalked outside, fully dressed and with her wand in her hand. She looked almost like her old self. Namely, furious. "What *did* you do? Did you just lock your aunt out of her own house?"

"She ran off and took Vanessa with her," I told her. "I figured that while she was gone, I could undo some of her handiwork, and there's a bunch of illegal potions in there that the police should be interested in too."

"She left town?" Her eyes narrowed. "When was this?"

"Chloe saw her a minute ago, but there's also a ghost on

its way here right now. I'm not joking." I looked to Chloe for backup, but she shrank away from the coven leader's wrath.

"I will find Shannon myself," said Mum. "As coven leader, that's my responsibility."

"What?" No way. "You just woke up from a coma."

She couldn't go off alone. If Aunt Shannon and Vanessa had already crossed the sage boundaries and the protective spells circling the town in their escape to the forest, she'd be right in the demon's path.

"I won't hear anything of it, Robin," she said. "If she fled on foot, she won't have gone far."

And she was gone, sweeping away with her cloak billowing behind her.

"Hey!" I ran after her retreating back. "Chloe—can you try to call the Head Witches? Or my brother?"

I didn't wait for an answer. Ramsey would be gathering his team, but I needed to find the Wardens too. Assuming they hadn't got far enough from the town to use transportation spells. *What is wrong with everyone?*

Mum was downright fast on her feet when she wanted to be, even after being in bed for weeks. My overflowing emotions had drawn a cloud of birds to circle overhead, but only a short distance into the forest, all birdsong vanished, and silence took its place.

Tansy clung to my shoulder and shivered. "It feels weird in here."

"Weird as in demons?" I didn't see Mum *or* Aunt Shannon, but the sage barrier, as far as I could tell, remained intact. Quickening my pace, I heard voices up ahead, and my heart lifted. "It's the Wardens."

As I ran towards the voices, Tam was the first to notice my approach and stopped in his tracks. Callum, Farley, and Perry did too.

"Hey." I jogged up to them. "Sorry my brother chased you off."

"You can't get rid of us that easily. Don't worry," said Perry. "Tam thinks there's something hiding here. In the forest."

A thrill of dread ran through my nerves. "He can sense it too?"

What kind of paranormal was he, anyway?

Tam inclined his head. "What do you mean too?"

"Tansy." I gestured to my familiar. "She can sense when there's a demon or something similar around because the wildlife all vanishes."

My own senses weren't so finely attuned, but the absence of birdsong was stark, and the shadows between the trees seemed deeper. *Mum. Where is she?*

"Yeah, I thought that was suspicious too," Callum said. "Did someone else come into the forest? I caught a few scents, but all of them were human."

"My aunt… she's fleeing town." Mum, though… dammit, she'd moved fast. I hadn't the faintest idea which direction she'd gone. "And my mother just woke up from a coma and decided to go after her. She shouldn't be wandering around alone, but good luck arguing with a coven leader on a mission."

Farley gasped. "A coma? From the demon?"

"No… the Reaper. I'll tell you later." We didn't have time to linger. "Anyway, she's awake now and wants to make up for lost time by seizing her wayward sister and dragging her back to town, regardless of whether there's a monster in the woods."

"Which way did they go?" asked Perry.

"Mum was just ahead of me, but…" I gestured helplessly to the forking paths. "I don't know."

"I'll pick up the scent," Callum offered, sniffing the air. "Someone else went… this way."

He took the lead, and Tansy scampered into step with him, also sniffing the path. The rest of us followed them deeper into the Wildwood.

"This is why I don't trust forests," Perry muttered. "What's that?"

My heart lurched when we rounded a corner and saw Callum sniffing at a body lying on the path. A human-sized body, which stirred as I approached and gave a distinct groan. "No…"

"Rowan!" I ran over and crouched beside her. She was covered in sticky webbing. "Are you all right?"

"Robin." She tried to roll over but didn't manage more than a twitch. "I'm sorry. I was trying to stop her from leaving."

Aunt Shannon. I pointed the sceptre at her and cast a reversal spell, which sent the webbing flying upward into a tree. "Did you see which way she went? My mum went after her."

"Your mum's really awake?" She shook off the sticky webs and climbed awkwardly to her feet. "After you left, I stayed near—near my mother's house. I just had a feeling, and when our grandmother's ghost came out of the house…"

"I'm sorry, what?" Perry said. "You have ghosts now?"

"Just the one, luckily." I beckoned to the Wardens. "This is my cousin. Rowan, these are the Wardens. They're supposed to be helping hunt the demon…"

"Oh—I'm Rowan. Robin's cousin. You're really hunting the demons? With what?" Rowan scanned their group as if she expected one of them to pull out a suitcase of monster-hunting gear, Ghostbusters style.

"With our wits and a ton of experience," Perry answered. "I'm Perry. This is Tam, Callum, and Farley, and normally, I'd have to force Maurice to introduce himself, too, but he got captured by your demon."

Rowan went pale. "The demon's here? In the forest?"

"If it isn't already in the forest, it will be soon," I told her. "And Aunt Shannon's most likely going to run straight into it."

"Oh no." Rowan bit her lip. "Do you need me to get backup? Ralph can fetch the police."

Perry recoiled when Ralph the tarantula emerged from Rowan's sleeve. "Is he your *familiar?*"

"Yes… why?"

"I don't like spiders."

"Don't you frequently fight demons?" Rowan queried.

"Demons usually have a sensible number of legs and eyes," Perry answered, backing away from the spider. "Please send him somewhere that isn't near me."

"Ramsey's supposed to be gathering the police anyway," I explained, "but otherwise, it's just us."

Someone screamed. All eyes turned in that direction, where thick trees masked the view. *Who was that?*

"Come on." Tam beckoned to his team, while I took off at a run too.

Tansy jumped up onto my shoulder, her little body shivering, as a familiar darkness enfolded the forest. *No. Not again.*

I ran faster, sceptre held high, a beacon through the darkness. Even the Wardens and Rowan had disappeared under the relentless dark. *This can't be just one demon...*

I tripped headlong over a body crouched behind a bush and landed on my knees. Curses flew in my direction, and through the haze, I spied Vanessa glowering at me from next to Aunt Shannon, also concealed in the bushes. Mum was nowhere to be seen.

"What are you doing?" I hissed at them.

"Are you going to help us or not?" Vanessa returned. "We're being hunted."

"Too bad," Tansy shot at her. "You left the safety of the town's boundaries behind. This is your problem."

"Tansy." She was right, but Mum was out here too. "Where is the monster?"

More to the point, where were the Wardens? The Wildwood was a veritable maze even without the darkness, and the afterworld's chill penetrated my clothes.

Mum's in here, and the last time she faced the dead in the forest, she ended up in a coma. I can't let that happen again.

I pointed the sceptre ahead of the bushes, its purple light illuminating the surrounding trees. "Whoever's out there, show yourself."

A growl came from the darkness, which coalesced around a spot on the path to my left, forming the shaggy outline of the ghast.

"Don't catch its attention!" Vanessa hissed.

"Little late." Hiding in the bushes wouldn't have done any good regardless, but she'd probably followed her mother's lead as usual. "I could use a hand."

As the beast advanced, I raised the sceptre and cast a freeze-frame spell, but that wouldn't last longer than a few seconds. *Where are the Wardens?* There weren't enough of us to properly banish the monster even if I included Perry and Farley, but maybe if we found Mum…

In a rustle of leaves, Aunt Shannon moved out of the bushes in a crouch, beckoning her daughter to follow. They backed away, down the path behind me. *Using me as a shield, are they?*

"Thanks for nothing." As the beast growled, I cast another freeze-frame spell and then pointed my sceptre upward. The eruption of purple light ought to draw the attention of anyone in the area… but would they get here in time?

"You can't win this, Head Witch," Vanessa said. "If we stay here, we'll die."

"I have to say I agree." A human-sized figure stepped out of the darkness beside the monster, shadows swirling downward to reveal a familiar face. Nothing had changed except her eyes, which were jet-black.

Leona.

15

Leona stood beside the beast she'd summoned. How she'd survived despite the deal she'd made with the demon was unclear, but more importantly, who was in the driver's seat? And just where were my allies? Aunt Shannon and Vanessa had continued their retreat through the bushes, though it wouldn't take more than a single leap for the monster to catch up to them.

Leona smiled at me. "It's been a while, Robin. Want to meet my other friends?"

"Not particularly."

The ghast was quite enough on its own without adding more monsters to the mix. Its huge shaggy form, coupled with the surrounding darkness, blotted out the sunlight that had been streaming through the trees, giving the illusion of us being in a cave.

"I'm sure some of your companions would like to meet one in particular." She took a step back, and a body fell forward out of the darkness. I recognised the pale features of an unconscious vampire. *Their missing teammate.*

"That wasn't nice of you either." Was the vampire even

alive? Well… technically, no, but I couldn't tell the difference between a regular vampire and a permanently dead one.

Tansy's fluffy tail tickled my ear. "I'll distract her."

I shook my head imperceptibly. The vampire had fallen out of the afterworld, suggesting more monsters lurked within that neither of us could see.

"I'll take the sage," Tansy pressed. "I can get them surrounded while their attention's on you."

"Fine," I breathed and felt her slide down my back to reach into my pocket.

At the same instant, the ghast shook off my freezing spell and leapt. I raised the sceptre and repeated my spell, knowing I was stalling, but what choice did I have? I couldn't banish this monster alone, to say nothing of the creature possessing Leona.

With the bag of sage in her mouth, Tansy kicked off from my shoulder and grabbed a lower branch, vanishing into the canopy above.

Leona lifted a brow. "Now your familiar's abandoned you?"

Believe whatever you like. I needed to keep her attention on me and make sure both she and the monster remained within the sage circle that Tansy was sneakily constructing. If that meant playing along with her, so be it.

"Just curious—how many people did you feed to the demon to avoid sacrificing your own life?" I asked Leona. "Have the benefits been worth it, or is the only upside that you're allowed to keep your life?"

I was curious, I'd admit, as to how much of Leona there was left in there. I didn't know the side effects of having a demon sharing your body in the long term, but I assumed they included losing what was left of one's humanity at the very least.

"I'm no longer helpless," she replied. "I'm stronger than you, Head Witch."

"Sure you are." Out of the corner of my eye, I spied Tansy making her stealthy way around the trees. I needed to make sure she wasn't spotted before she finished the circle. "What's the goal here? Why didn't you come back sooner?"

She'd been gathering allies, I'd assumed, but she hadn't brought all of them with her. That I could see, anyway. If I'd had a Reaper with me, I'd know, but I didn't. The forest, combined with the warped magic of the afterworld, had cut me off from the allies I did have, and while I was glad it was me left to face the monsters and not Mum, that didn't change how screwed I was.

Darkness swirled around Leona's feet. She made a sudden lunge forward—faster than any regular human—and grabbed Vanessa's arm, pulling my cousin in front of her like a shield.

"Let go of her!" Aunt Shannon's shrill voice echoed as she ran towards her older daughter, only for the ghast to bar her path.

I whipped the sceptre sideways with another short-lived freezing charm, but Leona's body language was clear. If I attacked her, Vanessa would die.

Rustling sounded above, and Tansy dropped onto my shoulder, whispering, "Done."

"Slight problem." Casting a banishment charm would put Vanessa's life at risk, and when she realised she was trapped in a sage circle, Leona might strike against my cousin anyway.

Aunt Shannon snarled. "If you let my daughter die, I will personally eviscerate you."

How pleasant. "What do you take me for?"

I might not have *liked* Vanessa, but I wasn't a monster. Instead of taking aim at Leona, I veered towards the ghast, which was also trapped within the circle. It was no longer a threat, but could I banish it myself? Doubtful.

"Did you think that trick would work?" Leona asked from behind a terrified Vanessa. "I have other allies too."

Darkness spread outward among the trees, forming a shaggy outline. Another ghost… and this one, given its location, was *not* trapped within the sage circle.

My heart sank. "Tansy… get out of here."

The beast leapt. Hot breath gusted in my face, and my freeze-frame spell stopped it before its teeth could reach me. I staggered, off-balance, and Tansy leapt from my shoulder. *What's she doing?*

Soaring in a flying arc, Tansy crashed into Leona's face and dug her claws in. Leona lifted her hands in an attempt to dislodge my familiar, which gave Vanessa a chance to flee once again.

"This way!" Her mother beckoned frantically, while I took aim at Leona's feet. I didn't dare cast too strong a spell in case Tansy got hurt, too, but the growling of a monster warned that the second beast had shaken off my spell.

I spun that way, but the beast's attention wasn't on me. A smaller but equally furry shape emerged from the bushes and crashed headlong into the monster, tackling it to the ground. A werewolf. That meant—

The other Wardens ran behind Callum, Tam in the lead, carrying some kind of wooden stick that must have been a weapon. Farley and Perry pointed their wands at the beast as it grappled with their teammate, but their spells had little effect.

"Damn, that thing's tough." Perry ran up to me. "Oh—and there's two of them now?"

"One's in a circle of sage," I told her. "Make sure nobody knocks it over."

"Oh." Perry gave a double-take at the sight of Leona. "And there's your demon?"

Leona scowled from behind the sage barrier, the beast at her side unable to move, either, but the other was more than strong enough to shake off the werewolf.

The monster advanced on Perry and Farley. I cast another immobilising charm, and the beast stopped inches from them, its paw frozen in midswipe.

"Thanks," Farley breathed. "Oh no—Maurice!"

She'd spotted the vampire lying prone on the forest floor. Tam approached on careful feet, stepping around the sage barrier without breaking it, and crouched over Maurice. "He's alive."

How can he tell? Vampires don't breathe. I was none the wiser as to what Tam was—he moved faster than a human and didn't carry a wand, but he had none of the other obvious supernatural abilities that a vampire did. Not that that was the pertinent issue right now.

Tansy jumped up to my shoulder. "Looks like your aunt did a runner again."

That figured. "We don't need her."

"Don't you?" Leona goaded from within the circle. "You're nothing but ordinary humans, whatever your abilities. You can't win."

"Not all of us are human," the vampire muttered into the undergrowth. "Do you always talk so much?"

"You *are* alive," Perry said.

"Don't need to sound that pleased," said Maurice, pushing onto his elbows. "What've we got here?"

"Two ghasts and a demon," Tam told him. "Don't try to move."

Maurice ignored him and climbed shakily to his feet. His gaze landed on the beast, which stirred beneath my freezing spell. "Let's deal with this one, Callum."

He darted behind the beast, and as it shook off the freezing spell, the ghast's lunge was cut off by the vampire slamming into it from behind, sending it pitching forward into the werewolf's claws. Tam joined them, swiping with that stick-like weapon of his, and the three swiftly drove the beast back.

"I think they've got that handled." Perry nodded to the circle. "Want to deal with them?"

"Not sure three of us will be enough," I muttered back. "Well… it's worth a try."

"Enough," Leona spat, sounding far more like a demon than a human. "That's enough games."

Darkness spilled across the ground, and another growl emanated from within it. *Not another one!*

"Watch out!" Perry grabbed the back of Farley's coat when she stumbled forward in the sudden rush of darkness. "Don't break the sage barrier."

Please don't. If the barrier was knocked aside, both would escape.

As the new arrival's huge paws solidified, Perry flicked her wand, casting a spell I belatedly recognised as a sleeping charm. The beast slumped sideways, only to blink a couple of times and recover.

"Okay… let's try again." Perry raised her wand, and this time, Farley did the same. Their spells hit the beast one after another, and its eyes slid closed.

"That won't work for long, fool," the demon goaded.

"What about this?" The vampire appeared behind Leona with his pointed teeth positioned over her neck. "Can a demon possess someone who's been drained of blood, I wonder?"

Good question. I risked a glance at Leona's face, which had frozen in a snarl. "Get away from me, vampire."

"I'm guessing the answer's no." Perry cast another spell on

the beast, which had begun to rise. "I'm also guessing you took care of that monster."

"That's right." Tam swung his stick-like weapon at the monster that had engaged Perry and Farley, and Callum's werewolf form followed close behind.

Abruptly, Leona fell forward, her body slumping in the vampire's arms. The demon rose upward like a cloud of smoke. *Did it let her go?*

"Now's our chance." Perry stepped to my side. "Banishment spell?"

"On three," Farley added. "One, two..."

I raised the sceptre. My own spell rippled outward, combining with their two smaller ones in a torrent that hit the demon head-on. Its dark form dissipated, becoming one with the shadows around Leona's still body. Too still.

Comprehension dawned. "It killed her."

"The demon sucked out her life force on the way out?" Perry asked. "Harsh, but that's what you get for teaming up with a demon."

"Yeah." I swivelled to the growling beast that remained trapped within the circle. "We need to deal with that too. What did your friends do to incapacitate the other one?"

"Not sure I want to know, to be honest. Werewolf teeth are sharp."

"Oh, we didn't permanently kill it," said Maurice, looking somewhat disappointed that his prey had dropped dead before he could drain her. "They're surprisingly tough."

Then someone needs to banish them.

"Move it to the sage circle," Tam told him. "We'll do the same with this one."

The vampire disappeared, while I helped Tam and Callum herd the second beast into the circle without knocking any of the sage askew. Once all three beasts were ensconced within the sage barrier, we had the slightly less achievable task of driving them out of this realm without the help of a Reaper.

"I hope Chloe reached the other Head Witches," I whispered to Tansy. "And Mum… I have to find her."

"There's someone over that way." Maurice pointed behind us. "I can hear them."

Vampire hearing must have often come in handy, though we'd caused enough of a racket in here that anyone would have been drawn to the sound of a fight. I hadn't gone far from the sage circle before I spied a single cloaked figure approaching. *Mum.*

Relief flooded me. "There you are."

"Robin." She halted, eyeing the sage circle. "Is that Leona?"

"The demon killed her on its way out," I said. "There are three ghasts. We can't banish them without backup."

"The police are on their way," she said. "I saw them when I was trying to find my way to you."

"You shouldn't have come." I swallowed more objections, my emotions a bitter cocktail of relief and resentment. "You should go home."

"Robin," Tansy said from the branch above my head. "He has Aunt Shannon."

"What?" I moved forward, rounded a corner, and spied Ramsey's team surrounding Vanessa and Aunt Shannon. "What are they doing?"

"You damaged the sage barrier around the town and endangered lives in the process," my brother was saying to Aunt Shannon as I approached. "I'm afraid I'm going to have to arrest you."

Was I dreaming? "Ramsey," I called to him. "She—wait, did you say she destroyed the sage barrier?"

"Part of it." He watched my approach, one eye on a surprisingly subdued Aunt Shannon. "My team found it on the way into the forest. Where's Leona?"

"Dead, and we have her monsters held captive in a sage circle," I replied. "What're you doing with those two?"

"My officers are going to bring them in."

"He's actually arresting them?" Tansy said.

"I think he just might be." Despite it all, I grinned. "It's about time."

16

Gloating wasn't becoming of a Head Witch, but watching the police escort Aunt Shannon and Vanessa away was among the most satisfying experiences of my life. My euphoria lasted until my brother approached me alone. "Robin, why did you let our mother come into the forest?"

"You're seriously blaming me for that?" I could have hit him. "You know she does whatever she wants."

I glanced behind me at Mum herself, who approached us. "Robin, I do hope you didn't plan to leave those monsters unattended for long."

"The Wardens are watching them," I said for my brother's benefit. "We need to banish them, but there aren't enough of us."

"Robin!" Rowan came running over. "I got lost in the forest. Where's…?"

"Leona is dead," I told her. "The demon finished her off on the way out. Also, your mother and sister are on their way to jail."

Conflicting emotions crossed her face until they settled

on a smile. "Good."

"I'll see if Chloe managed to call any of the other Head Witches," I said. "And gather the coven."

"No, I will," Mum said. "The coven needs to hear from me."

I decided against objecting. While the ghasts were less threatening while encased in a circle of sage, I didn't like the thought of them lurking outside of our borders, and Mum would be safer with the coven than here in the woods.

Without the darkness of the afterworld shrouding the path, it didn't take long until we found our way to the exit. My phone signal must have been blocked, because a flurry of messages showed up when we left the forest. At a guess, Piper and Harvey were trying to get hold of me. I hadn't had time to warn them. I'd had so little warning myself. I'd have to deal with that later, because Mum was on a mission. She hadn't even objected to the police carting her sister off to jail, and she ignored Ramsey's and my attempts to steer her towards home and instead made for the coven headquarters.

So did I, mostly to see if Chloe was around. I assumed she'd returned to the office to call the other Head Witches, but when I opened the door, there was no sign of her or of Grandma. Weird, but maybe she'd gone somewhere else to make the call.

As I backed out of the office, Tansy waved at me from the doorway. "The Wardens are leaving."

"They're doing what?" I ran after my familiar, down the street to the spot where the remaining Wardens had gathered.

"Robin," Tam called to me. "Sorry, but we've been called to another job. I gather it's urgent."

"Already?" I frowned. "Aren't two of your people still in the woods?"

"They are," Perry ventured. "What job is this? Can't it

wait?"

"Some kind of local emergency," Tam said. "It sounds serious, though. I said we'll see what we can do."

"Not until we're rid of those monsters," said Farley. "Isn't that the important thing here?"

"Robin." Mum walked out of the headquarters behind me. "Can you explain why none of the coven members are in their offices?"

"No." What was going on? "Maybe Chloe warned them something was going on in the forest. I can't find her either. She was supposed to be calling the other Head Witches so we can banish those monsters..."

I trailed off when I saw Callum and Maurice approaching from the forest, joining their teammates.

"Aren't you supposed to be watching the ghasts?" Perry asked.

"The Reaper banished them." Callum nodded to me. "Your friend, right?"

"Friend?" My gaze snapped to my phone, but Maura's name wasn't there among the people who'd been trying to get hold of me.

It's not her.

Foreboding seized me. "Something's wrong. What's this emergency, Tam?"

"A prison break."

Oh. Oh no.

"I know who it is." I took in a breath. "We're all in danger. We have to get out of here."

"Too late." The clear voice rang out from the path leading to the forest. A slight figure approached us, her curly hair bouncing to her shoulders and her steps followed by the faint shadows of the afterworld.

Linnea gave me a wide smile, as humourless as a demon. "Hello again, Robin Wildwood."

ABOUT THE AUTHOR

Elle Adams lives in the middle of England, where she spends most of her time reading an ever-growing mountain of books, planning her next adventure, or writing. Elle's books are humorous mysteries with a paranormal twist, packed with magical mayhem.

She also writes urban and contemporary fantasy novels as Emma L. Adams.

Visit http://www.elleadamsauthor.com/ to find out more about Elle's books.

9 781916 584112